*W*HEN *coffee and brandy were set before them, Nico turned to the subject of his cousin.*

"I know Leon has said he wishes to marry you. No doubt he has also told you he will let nothing stand in his way. Leon has fallen in love so many times in the past that I know his lines by heart."

"Are you also implying he will fall in love many more times in the future?" Alex questioned.

"I do not know that," Nico said. "His love for you may well be the first genuine emotion he has experienced. You are beautiful enough to arouse such feelings in a man."

"I'm not in love with him," Alex insisted, "and I have no intention of marrying him."

Nico said nothing but there was a brooding quality in his face that suggested he was trying to assess her words. Watching him, it suddenly became important for her to make him believe her. . . .

Night of Love

Roberta Leigh

FAWCETT GOLD MEDAL • NEW YORK

NIGHT OF LOVE

© 1978 Roberta Leigh

Published by Fawcett Gold Medal Books, a unit of CBS Publications, the Consumer Publishing Division of CBS Inc.

A selection of the Doubleday Romance Library Book Club.

ISBN: 0-449-14071-7

Printed in the United States of America

10 9 8 7 6 5 4 3 2 1

To E.M.L. and J.H.L.
The two who matter most.

The approbation of the public I consider as the greatest reward of my labours; but am determin'd to regard its judgement, whatever it be, as my best instruction.

David Hume   (1739)

Night
of Love

Chapter One

The invitation from Eleanor Dean could not have come at a better time, and Alex Godfrey wondered if her godmother was psychic. How else could she have known it was imperative for her goddaughter to leave the smog of a British winter for a sunnier clime?

Alex sighed heavily, then pulled a face, for the deep breath brought with it a familiar pain in her chest. According to her doctor, there was no reason for the pain to be there; the patch on her lung, caused by a bronchial cold that had led to pneumonia, had long since cleared up, and any pain she suffered was purely psychosomatic. But psychosomatic or not, she knew it was more than nerves that made it impossible for her to gain the seven pounds she had lost, or to sleep through a night without waking up gripped by a nameless terror. There was no doubt a few months in the sunshine—even the wintery sunshine of Provence— would be a great improvement on February in London.

Afraid that if she hesitated too long before accepting the invitation, she might be offered a job that would then make it impossible for her to get away, she immediately wrote her godmother a letter of acceptance.

"At the moment I'm in a state euphemistically known as resting," she confessed, "though you would no doubt call it being out of work! A holiday in France is exactly what I need, and a million thanks for suggesting it. Expect me some time towards the end of the week."

Alex's flatmate, Sherry Dickson, was delighted yet dismayed at the prospect of her friend's departure. "This place will be like a morgue without you."

"I'll only be away a month. Anyway, once you start rehearsals for your new play, you won't have time to miss me."

"Yes I will. I'll have no one to nag!"

"Can't you get someone to stay with you?"

"If you're worried about your share of the rent," Sherry said, "forget it. My agent got me such a good contract—"

"No charity," Alex interrupted. "I can afford to pay my way even though I *am* out of work. I only suggested you have someone here because I know you don't like living alone."

"I could ask Jane," Sherry mused. "She loathes her bed-sitter. But you'd have to give me a week's warning before you came back. I couldn't throw her out until she'd found another place."

"Suits me," Alex agreed. "I doubt if I'll need to

rush back home for a star part! Producers haven't been beating a path to my door."

"The more fools they," Sherry said staunchly. "Your acting's as good as your looks, and you know how stunning *they* are."

"Pity you aren't in charge of casting," Alex grinned. "Beautiful blondes are still expected to play vamps, and short of dyeing my hair brown. . . ."

"Don't you dare! You'll get a break one day. I feel it in my bones."

Though touched by her friend's fervor, Alex was too realistic to let herself be swayed by it. What counted was the use she could make of her looks and talent, and, since leaving drama school, this had amounted to two years' slog in a repertory company and a week's run in a disastrous West End play, which had culminated in the pneumonia that had now left her financially and physically depleted.

"Sometimes I think I'm mad not to take up another career," she murmured. "Acting's so damned precarious."

"Why not give it up and retire into marriage? Frank Paddock's asked you often enough."

"I don't love him."

Sherry sighed. "You're still looking for a father figure. I suppose it's because your real one died when you were a kid."

Alex shrugged and wished she had a stronger recollection of the army colonel who had been killed on maneuvers, bequeathing her only his name and his tall, blond good looks. Of her mother she had no memory whatever, for she had died in childbirth, leaving her daughter to be brought up by a succession of nannies and finally her godmother, Eleanor Dean.

"It's strange," she murmured, "but even now I find it hard to understand why Eleanor never married. As a child I always had the impression that the house was full of young men—with lots of laughter and love."

"She was too wrapped up in her journalism," Sherry replied. "I still can't figure out why she packed it in and went to France."

"She thought a more restful life would be better for her arthritis."

"Do you think she regrets the move?"

"She's never said so. But then she isn't the type to complain." Alex frowned. "I feel guilty for not going to see her since she left, but it's too far to go for a weekend, and this past year I've been too busy to take a holiday."

"You can make up for it now." Sherry put two coffee cups on a tray. "If you like it there, why not stay for the summer? If there's any sign of work I can always send you a cable."

"I'll see how I feel."

"You might even meet some handsome Frenchman. Those dark Latins always go for blondes."

"I'm more likely to meet a pig farmer! According to Eleanor, Cabray is a tiny village in the hills."

"Let me keep a few illusions," Sherry pleaded. "And marrying you off to a wealthy aristocrat has always been one of them!"

"I won't find him in Provence," Alex laughed.

"I've a psychic feeling you will."

"Direct your psychic feelings to the kettle. It's boiling over!"

On a flurry of laughter, the conversation ended.

Exactly a week later Alex leaned out of the window of her small bedroom and looked down on a landscape that could have been painted by Cézanne. It had the same limpid, blue-green quality, and the trees, bare of leaves, showed the beauty and form of the branches. For miles around, fields and trees and gently undulating hills mingled one with the other, the land rising and falling in graceful curves until it reached the edge of the horizon, where it rose sharply into craggy boulders. Here the color changed too, the silver-green becoming lilac before it melded into a pale blue, cloudless sky.

Idly her eyes roamed the nearby fields, picking out a narrow, winding road on which glinted the windscreen of a solitary car, its wheezing engine clearly heard in the silent air. Closer at hand a young priest on a bicycle, his long black skirts flapping 'round the wheels, cycled purposefully towards a stone cottage a quarter of a mile away. The house belonged to her godmother's nearest neighbor, a professor of uncertain age and temper who, like Eleanor, had retired to the village in search of peace and quiet.

They had certainly found it, Alex conceded, closing the window against the sharp east wind, for though things had changed in the past few years—chiefly a drastic increase in the cost of living—the solitude had remained. But now this was suddenly being threatened, for yesterday the young priest had stopped by to tell them that Monsieur Brun, a young farmer with an increasing family, had obtained permission to turn one of his fields into a camping site and was, at this moment, making all the necessary arrangements for sewage, electricity, and water.

"He won't get young campers coming here," Eleanor had commented when she heard the news. "They prefer to be near the coast."

"Let's hope you're right," the priest had replied. "It will be better for the village if the campers are older. At least they won't make so much noise."

"Where will they do their shopping?" Alex had asked, thinking of the tiny village with its limited supplies.

"Monsieur Duvat is already talking about enlarging his shop, and the baker has ordered an electric oven."

"He won't be getting *my* custom, then," Eleanor had said sharply. "All you get from an electric oven is nasty aerated cotton wool!"

Alex remembered this as she went down the narrow stone stairs to the surprisingly large living room that, apart from a small kitchen, comprised the entire ground floor of the cottage. A massive stone fireplace took up the whole of the far wall, and from a wooden beamed ceiling hung several gleaming copper pots. Rugs were scattered on the red tiled floor, while several easy chairs, covered in oatmeal tweed, gave an indication of the smart Chelsea house where they had originated.

Looking at Eleanor Dean as she emerged from the kitchen bearing two mugs of coffee, it was difficult to envisage her in an urban setting, so much at home did she look in this rustic one. A farmer's wife without a farm, Alex thought with amusement, as her godmother went to the window and rapped on the pane to frighten away several inquisitive chickens who had come to scratch around on the terrace outside.

"I'll have to get the hen house repaired," the woman muttered. "If I'd thought of it, I'd have asked Father Pierre if he could recommend someone for me. It's such a bore not being able to bend. You'd think my arthritis would have improved in this climate—not got worse."

There was nothing reassuring that Alex could say. Indeed, she had been hard pressed not to show how dismayed she was by her godmother's greater frailty. Had the arthritis become worse because of financial worries? Stress could play strange tricks in illness, and, if this were the case here, it was not surprising her godmother's health was failing, for she made no secret that it was becoming hard to live on the annuity with which she had retired to Cabray.

"Why don't you sell up and come back to London and live with me?" Alex asked aloud.

"Young people should live alone."

"Young people don't want to live alone."

"So who's your boyfriend?" her godmother asked.

"I haven't got one!"

"It can't be for lack of offers."

"It isn't," Alex admitted, "but I've been too busy concentrating on my career."

"It might have helped your career!"

"The casting couch, you mean?" Alex smiled. "I never fancied getting my success that way."

"What about real love? The old-fashioned kind?"

"I've never found it." Alex shrugged. "Maybe I never will."

"You've too much awareness to go through life untouched," her godmother said. "When the right man comes along you'll go overboard for him."

"What an awful thought." Alex went to the door. "How about going into the Cabray village? I'd like to find out if anyone is opposing the caravan site."

"They'll all be welcoming it," Eleanor Dean said drily. "You aren't in rural England, my dear. French peasants will promote anything that puts money in their pockets!"

Alex soon discovered the truth of this assertion, for the villagers were delighted at the prospect of having tourists during the summer months. There were varying reports as to the number of caravans Monsieur Brun was allowed on his site, ranging from twenty to as many as a hundred. Taking a middle figure, it still meant a large influx of money coming into the village and, returning home laden with provisions, Alex had the beginning of an idea that might well route some of it into her godmother's pockets. It would mean a lot of hard work, of course, and she herself would have to stay here until it was properly organized. But once the scheme was set up, it would be possible to keep it going with outside help from the village.

"The campers won't want to be bothered cooking the whole time," she explained to her godmother over lunch. "And if we could offer them toasted snacks and some of your fabulous cakes, I'm sure they'd be delighted."

"I couldn't cope with the work," Eleanor said flatly.

"I'd help you."

"You're here for a rest."

"I'm already rested."

"No." It was a firm sound. "I couldn't let you."

"Why not? It's the sort of challenge I like."

"For how long? Or do I pack it in when you go back to London?"

"I'll stay here until I get a job offered to me. Then I'd find you someone to take my place. I'm sure one of the women in the village would jump at the chance of earning extra money."

Eleanor Dean still looked uncertain, and Alex, afraid her offer might be seen as a sacrifice, was prompted to say:

"It would do me good to remain here for the summer. And it won't matter to my career if I drop out of sight for a season. Anyway, there's little chance of going into a new play until the autumn."

"Your talents are being wasted in London, and they'll certainly be wasted here," came the tart reply.

"Maybe I don't have any talents."

"If that's what you think, you should change your profession."

"I *am* changing it—temporarily. I'm planning to start work at Ye Olde Village Tea Shoppe!"

"You're really set on the idea, aren't you?"

"What have we got to lose?"

"A fair bit of money and a great deal of energy." Eleanor Dean flung out an arm in capitulation. "Don't say I haven't warned you."

"I won't," Alex smiled. "And I'll remind you of your pessimism when we start banking the cash!"

Chapter Two

*In the backbreaking weeks that fol-*lowed, Alex wondered if she would have put forward her suggestion had she known the effort it would entail.

Because money was short, she and her godmother did all the preparation themselves. This involved making several rustic tables and benches; laying a narrow gravel path from the rickety front gate across the uneven lawns to the terrace that ran along the front of the cottage; and improving the terrace itself by scrubbing the flagstones with acid to get rid of the mossy fungus that made it slippery to walk on.

Slowly the atmosphere of decay was replaced by one of charm, increased by the large earthenware pots trailing fronds of early geraniums, which Monsieur Brun delivered to them one morning as a present.

Only the kitchen remained a problem they could not solve with their hands, and transforming it required a necessary dipping into their financial resources. But even here they did it the cheapest way: ignoring the splendid shops and attending numerous auctions in Grasse and Nice, where they obtained two electric grills and all the china and cutlery they needed. Their only new item was an electric mixer which Alex insisted on buying her godmother as a present.

"I intended to get you one before I returned to England," she said, refusing to be paid, "so I'm only giving it to you in advance."

It was a gift that Eleanor immediately put to use, experimenting with various recipes for scones and cakes, each batch more delicious than the last.

"I'd better not eat any of your cakes myself," Alex grinned, "or the only stage part I'll be asked to play will be the fat lady in a circus!"

"You won't have any weight problems once you start running after customers." Eleanor looked at her goddaughter's supple figure. "You're still too thin for my liking. You haven't lost those hollows in your neck—they're deep as salt cellars."

"I think they make me look ethereal!" Alex peered at herself in the pine-framed mirror that hung on the wall nearby.

The hard physical work of the past few weeks might not have made her stronger, but it had left her with little time to worry about her career or why she had not heard from her agent since she had left England. Sometimes she found it hard to believe she had been away two months. She smoothed her hair back from her forehead. Even in this twilight hour it was the color of golden corn, with here and there a glint of silver-gilt to highlight a wayward curl.

"I'll have to wear it away from my face when I'm serving food," she muttered. "How about a pony tail?" She pulled it back and swung round to look at her godmother.

"It makes you look sixteen."

"Is that good or bad?"

"Depends how you want to look."

"Industrious and capable," Alex said promptly. "Then I won't attract roving eyes!"

"You'll never be able to avoid them."

"I intend to try."

With this in mind, she sorted through her clothes that night to find something suitable to the image she wished to project. A plain cotton frock seemed the best answer. They needed the custom of the quieter holidaymaker rather than the younger, more boisterous one.

She wandered over to the window and peered into the garden. The tables and benches they had labored to make stood sturdily on the terrace; the grass had been clipped short and the worst of the weeds removed. Nothing could make the garden look well tended, but at least it no longer resembled a wilderness. If things went well, they might be able to afford someone to take care of it. But for the moment, all she could do was pray Monsieur Brun's campers would take note of the carefully worded notice she had pinned to the bulletin board he had erected by the entrance gate of his caravan site. If they didn't, then all the work she and Eleanor had done would be wasted.

May came in with a rush of sunny days, and by the

fifth one, Monsieur Brun's camping field was dotted with caravans. The village had prepared itself too, and though the grocery store had not yet been enlarged, two counters had been hastily put up beside the front door, to hold fresh fruit and vegetables and leave more room inside for the dry goods.

It was here that everyone gathered to learn the local news, the place where Alex herself was always brought up to date with the happenings in Cabray.

"According to gossip," she informed her godmother, "the caravaners are middle-aged and not averse to spending money. I only hope some of them start spending it here."

"We'll probably have a lot of food left over during the first couple of weeks," Eleanor warned. "Even with a fridge, we can't keep anything for more than two days."

"Then we should concentrate on biscuits and nutty things that won't go bad. And we needn't prepare any snacks until they're actually ordered."

"We'll have to prepare a *few* things in advance," Eleanor protested. "Some people will refuse to wait long."

After giving it careful thought, they filled the refrigerator with assorted dips and pureed vegetables which, with the addition of cream or milk, could quickly be turned into delicious soups or made into fillings for sandwiches.

"Now we sit back and wait," Alex said. "Once the novelty of taking care of themselves has worn off, we should have a few arriving for a midmorning nosh-up!"

Her prophesy came true, and, on the second day, three separate families presented themselves for coffee and cakes, with one of them announcing they would come back for tea.

By the end of the week Alex and her godmother were so exhausted that when evening came they barely had the energy to swallow their supper and climb the stairs to bed. Yet despite the work, they were both mentally relaxed; Alex could barely conceal her delight and Eleanor seemed to have fewer aches and pains or else was too busy to be aware of them.

Their happiest time came on Sunday evening when the takings for the week were added up and their expenditure subtracted, they found they had made sufficient profit for Eleanor not to withdraw her usual weekly sum of money from the bank.

"We haven't counted what we've spent on the furnishings, though," the older woman cautioned as Alex danced round the sitting room waving a fistful of French francs.

"But this is only the first week," Alex enthused. "By the end of the month, we'll be completely in the black. You've got to admit it was a brainwave of mine."

"It was a wonderful idea," Eleanor said warmly. "And it means you won't have to go back to London empty-handed. We'll go fifty-fifty on the profits."

"No we won't."

"Yes we will."

"No." Alex was adamant. "I'm living here rent free, and it isn't costing me a bean for my food. The least I can do in return is to set you up in business!" Her mouth curved slightly. "You know, I'm not sure I *want* to go back to London. I'm loving it here."

"Wait till Sherry wires you there's a job in the offing!"

"I still don't think I'll want to rush back. I enjoy watching people eat. It must be some maternal instinct in me!"

"Then hurry up and find a husband."

"I'll put up a sign next to the tea and snacks," Alex grinned. "I rather fancy myself marrying a local yokel!"

May drew to a close, and the hedgerows were ablaze with honeysuckle, wild roses, and magnificent purple bougainvillea. The land around the cottage bloomed in such wild beauty that Alex wished she had the time and knowledge to cultivate it. But the customers seemed to like its wildness, saying it added to the unspoiled charm of the surroundings.

Eleanor was less sanguine about the dilapidation, especially when a young child fell down the crumbling steps that led from one terraced lawn to another.

"If we don't get a few repairs made," she remarked one evening, "someone will get badly injured and sue us. That balustrade on the side of the terrace has to be fixed, too. I'll have a word with Auguste."

"One of your beaux?" Alex asked.

"A beefy one," came the reply. "He's the local butcher! He has two sons who occasionally do odd jobs."

"I'd hardly call the repairs you want an odd job! You'd do better to try and get someone from Grasse."

"They'd charge more."

"Then wait a bit. There's no point spending more money until we're sure the whole thing's going to work."

Many months later Alex was to remember the advice she had given Eleanor and to wonder how differ-

ent the course of her life would have been had she not
prevented her godmother from having the terrace repaired.

The morning after their discussion, Alex awoke to a
grey and windy world. Rain was flattening the grass,
and the wind set the tables and chairs swaying in protest.

"It looks as if we're in for a profitless day," she
said as she came down to breakfast.

"Spoken like a true capitalist!" Eleanor passed
across a plate of hot croissants. "But I've known worse
days than this to turn sunny before noon."

"Not this one," Alex replied, and she was immediately proved wrong by the appearance of a watery
sun and a startlingly beautiful rainbow across the sky.

Enchanted by the sight, she stared at it for a long
while, reminded of the colored spotlights that illu-
minated a stage. Her life in the theater seemed a
world away, and she wondered if she had lost her
desire to be an actress. Would she be content to live
here permanently with her godmother, working long,
hectic hours during the summer and relaxing in the
winter, or would she—once her full vitality returned
—be driven by a restlessness to return to her career?
Her brows, delicately arched and several shades darker
than her golden hair, came together in a frown. That
she could even consider giving up the stage suggested
she had undergone some change. A year ago such an
idea would never have entered her head. With an
effort, she forced herself to stop thinking of the future.
Time enough for that in the autumn—or if Sherry
sent her a cable telling her to return to London.

By noon the wind and rain had died completely,

and a few holidaymakers straggled in for coffee. By the time they were served, more people had arrived, and for the next hour Alex was kept busy running between the terrace and the kitchen.

"If things go on like this," Eleanor grumbled, staring at the mound of dirty crockery, "we'll have to buy a dishwasher."

"Let's go to Nice tomorrow morning," Alex urged. "If we—"

"Ma'm'selle!"

A man's voice made Alex swing round sharply to see a dark-skinned man by the door.

"Forgive me," he began, "but I've been waiting outside, and—"

"I'll be with you in a moment," she interrupted.

"I only want—"

"A moment, monsieur," Alex said even more firmly. "Then I'll come out and take your order."

"But—"

With a loud clatter she set some crockery on to a tray, and, taking the hint, the man hastily withdrew. But as she came out of the back door she found him waiting for her, and he followed on her heels as she moved past him to serve the waiting customers. Only when she had done so did she return to where he was standing.

"I'm sorry about the delay," she said coldly, "but I'm the only one serving, and I have to take customers in their order."

"But I don't want to order!" he exclaimed. "I merely wish to have some water for my Ferrari."

"Your what?"

"My car. The radiator has overheated. I was obliged to park it at the top of the lane."

"Oh dear, I *am* sorry." Although contrite, she could not help being amused and was glad when he smiled back at her.

"I'm not a bit sorry," he replied. "In fact I'm delighted with my car. Had it not overheated, I would never have met you."

His look of admiration was bold, and her amusement lessened.

"How much water do you want?"

"A bucketful, I suppose."

"I'll fetch it for you."

"You must let *me* do it."

He accompanied her to the kitchen and watched as she filled a bucket in the sink. He stepped forward to pull it out and walked off gingerly with it, careful not to spill any on his elegant beige slacks.

"Nice-looking young man," Eleanor commented.

"I didn't notice," Alex said.

"He noticed *you*."

Alex shrugged and returned to the terrace. She was busy clearing the tables when she saw him returning across the grass, tall, dark, and definitely not English, for he had spoken with a slight accent that she found difficult to place.

"One empty bucket duly returned," he smiled and looked at an empty table. "Is it too late for me to order some coffee?"

"Of course not."

"Will you join me?"

"I'm afraid I can't; we're still busy."

"I'm not. I can easily wait for you."

"It could be a long wait."

"No wait is long when there's a pretty girl at the end of it!"

"Are you a horticulturist?" she asked.

He looked blank, then shook his head. "Why do you ask?"

"Because your compliments are so flowery!"

He was still smiling when she returned a few minutes later with his order. He had not asked for cakes but she had brought some, and he eyed them with interest.

"They look homemade and excellent."

"They are both!"

He picked one up. "How long has this cottage been a café?" he asked.

"We've only just opened."

"We?"

"My godmother and myself. The cottage is hers. I'm only here for a holiday."

"It doesn't *look* like a holiday." He took a biscuit and bit into it with large white teeth. "Excellent," he pronounced and finished the rest of it.

Alex moved off to give some Germans their bill, and by the time this was done, the remaining customers had gone too, leaving only the dark-haired young man.

"Will you join me for a coffee now?" he asked as she made to move past him.

Deciding it was churlish to refuse, she fetched another cup and some more fresh coffee.

"If you offer two lots of fresh coffee to your customers," he smiled, "you won't make much profit!"

She smiled back. "You're very knowledgeable about the restaurant business."

"I am knowledgeable about *business*. It's the Greek in me!"

So he was a Greek; she should have guessed. She glanced at him quickly and then looked away, but not before he had seen the gesture.

"My name is Leonardis Panos." He stood up and half bowed. "And you are?"

"Alex Godfrey."

"Alex. That's an unusual name. You are Greek too? But no, with such fair hair it would be impossible." He gave her a speculative stare. "How long are you staying here?"

"I'm not sure. Perhaps all summer."

His dark eyes rested on her ringless hands. "There is no man to object?"

"No." She pushed back her chair and rose, and at once he did the same.

"I have the feeling you are running away from me," he said.

"I have work to do."

"What time do you finish? I am hoping you will have dinner with me."

"You're a fast worker."

"That should go down well with a hard-working one!"

She could not help laughing, and he took it as acceptance of his invitation.

"What time shall I collect you, Alex?"

She hesitated, still not sure whether to say yes. Yet why shouldn't she accept his offer? It was a long time since she had gone out with a man, and this one looked as if he could be amusing. Flirtatious but amusing.

"I'll be ready at eight," she said and began to clear his table, pausing only to watch as he went down the steps to the gate.

As she had anticipated, he stopped there and turned to wave, and she waved back, suddenly pleased at the prospect of seeing him again. Leonardis Panos. The name had a familiar ring, though she could not place it. He was a Greek and obviously rich if he could afford to drive a Ferrari. Apart from that, he was a mystery. The thought lent excitement to the evening ahead, and she had a strong presentiment it was going to be the first evening of many.

Chapter Three

Alex stared reflectively at the contents of her wardrobe and decided to wear something casual. Better to look understated than give the impression she was trying too hard. She slipped into a pleated silk dress the same color as her corn-gold hair. The skirt swung 'round her shapely legs, and the close-fitting bodice subtly revealed the contours of her firm, big breasts and small waist.

"You look beautiful," Eleanor stated as she came into the living room. "I'm glad you accepted Mr. Panos's invitation."

"I feel guilty at leaving you."

"I'm used to being alone."

"Now you're making me feel worse!"

Eleanor chuckled. "That wasn't my intention. It was only my way of saying I enjoy the rut I'm in!"

The throb of an engine made them both glance through the window, and Alex saw the gleam of headlights in the darkness of the lane.

"I'm glad there's a moon," she commented. "It can be tricky walking from the gate to the house at night."

"I keep meaning to have a couple of lights fixed along the path."

"That *is* an odd job," Alex grinned. "I'll allow you to ask the butcher's son to do *that!*"

Footsteps rang out on the terrace and she went to open the front door. Leonardis Panos came in. He was still wearing beige, but a suit this time, with a sharply cut jacket and a cream shirt and tie that heightened the darkness of his skin. Now that she was wearing high heels, Alex saw he was only a few inches taller than herself, though he stood very straight, as if conscious of his lack of height. As he came forward, she smelt his shaving lotion, subtle and musky and more feminine than masculine. But there was nothing feminine about the look he gave her. If ever a look undressed a girl, that one did. She lowered her eyes to hide her amusement.

"You are even lovelier than I remembered," he murmured, and, coming forward, he noticed Eleanor by the fireplace. He was in no way put out at knowing he had been overheard, and he stepped over to greet her.

"You are the godmother? I hope you will forgive me for taking Alex away from you for the evening."

"I'm delighted she's going out. She's been working far too hard for too long."

"I will do my best to see she relaxes." He looked at Alex. "I have booked a table for us at La Reserve."

His tone assumed she knew it, but she deliberately looked at him with blankness in her eyes. She had never been to any of the expensive restaurants along the coast and had no intention of pretending she had.

"It is a hotel in Beaulieu," he explained, "with wonderful food." He replaced the cardigan that was threatening to slip from her shoulders. "Do you have something warmer? I am driving with the top down."

"I'll get my coat."

She returned from her room wearing the only coat she had brought with her: a light tweed in a mixture of green and blue. Bidding Eleanor goodnight, she followed her escort to his car. He did not turn it 'round but backed it at hair-raising speed up to the main road. Once there, he set off for the coast as if the devil was at his heels.

Alex sank lower in the seat. Surprisingly it was not cold, for the windscreen acted as a shield, and she only felt a slight breeze ruffle the top of her head as the hedgerows flashed past.

"Do you always drive so fast?"

"Don't you like it?"

"Not much."

Immediately he slowed to a crawl. "I never notice what speed I'm doing."

"I hope you don't tell that to your insurance company!"

"It wouldn't matter if I did. It's our own."

She gave him a swift glance. He was staring intently ahead, and she was convinced he was totally unaware how conceited his remark had sounded. For the second time she wondered where she had heard the name Panos and determined to ask him.

"We're in shipping," he explained. "Shipping and Greeks. They go together like bread and butter!"

She laughed. "Do all Greeks make their money in shipping?"

"All the ones the public are likely to hear about. The Panoses have many other interests, too."

She wondered to whom "the Panoses" referred. Perhaps it was his father and brothers; even uncles and cousins. Greeks were family-oriented, she knew, and if one of them was a success, he generally employed all the other males in the family.

"We are not like many of the wealthy Greek families you have read about," he continued. "We didn't go from rags to riches in a single lifetime. Our position has been secure and established for many generations."

"Only in Greece or around the world?"

"Everywhere. Yet Greece remains our home." He half turned to look at her. "We've talked enough about me. Tell me about yourself. What do you do, besides wait on tables?"

"I'm an actress."

"Ah." It was a pleased sound. "Should I have heard of you?"

"Not unless you saw any repertory plays in Leeds! I'm afraid I haven't made my mark in the West End of London."

"Don't tell me you want to see your name in lights? You're too lovely to waste your time pleasing an audience. You should be pleasing one man only."

"Some people would say that's an even bigger waste of time!"

"Do you agree?"

"At the moment."

They negotiated a bend, and she saw the lights of the coast far below. They were descending fast, and the air was becoming perceptibly warmer.

"Another fifteen minutes and we'll be there," the man at the wheel said. "Luckily auto routes make nonsense of distance."

"Do you have good roads in Greece?"

"Fair. But I am not there much. For the past three years, I've lived in New York. I came to France because Nico wants me to run the Paris office."

"Nico?"

"My cousin. He is Uncle Christoff's only son. One day he will inherit the whole empire."

"You make him sound like a Prince."

"He's probably more important! When you're a billionaire, you have enormous influence. And he knows how to use it. Everything he touches turns to gold."

"Midas wasn't a happy man."

"Then he didn't know how to enjoy his money. My uncle and Nico do. They both work hard and play hard. At least my uncle did when he was young. Now he only works!"

"Do you have any brothers and sisters?" she asked, more for want of something to say than because she cared.

"One sister. She is married to a Greek-American."

"Greeks always marry Greeks, don't they?"

"Usually. Personally, I think it is nonsense. The world is too small for nationalities and races to remain segregated."

"I'm not sure I agree. If we all intermarried, the human race would become one great big pudding. At the moment, the differences between people makes for interest."

"As well as racial prejudice and war," he added. "But why are we talking so seriously? I should be telling you how happy I am that my car broke down this morning. If it hadn't, I would never have met you."

"You've already told me that."

"But you didn't believe me!" He caught her hand. "Finding you in Cabray made me feel like a prospector finding a gold nugget in the desert! You really are a golden girl. The first thing I noticed about you was your hair, and—"

"Are those the lights of Beaulieu?" she cut across his fulsome compliments, and, recognizing her wish to change the subject, he nodded and pointed out a few landmarks as they bowled down the steep road to the narrow one that ran along the coast.

On their right lay the harbor, large and filled with opulent yachts, while beyond it one glimpsed the sea, dark and shining like black satin. A hundred yards along, they turned into the entrance of La Reserve and were soon sitting in the bar, a bottle of champagne in a silver bucket in front of them.

"To you, my fair Alex." Leon raised his glass to her. "And to the beautiful music we will make together."

She sipped her champagne and ignored his toast, knowing it was futile to protest at it. Leon was a man who would only understand actions, and she would allow these to speak for her when the time came. But not until he himself resorted to action. The prospect of fighting an amorous Greek in a car was not an enjoyable one, and she pushed it aside. She was old enough to take care of herself, and she mustn't let it stop her from enjoying her evening with this good-looking young man.

But as the hours passed, she was not sure how enjoyable his company really was, for though he talked continuously, he said nothing particularly interesting. He had a butterfly mentality and flitted from subject to subject as he no doubt flitted from girl to girl.

"How is it you aren't married?" she asked during a momentary lull in his conversation. "I thought Greek men marry young."

"The women do," he explained. "Not the men. They like to sow their wild oats for a long time."

"How old-fashioned that sounds!"

"We are an old-fashioned people."

"You mean you don't sow wild oats once you're married?"

"Only occasionally! And in *our* family, we have Uncle Christoff to deal with if we overstep ourselves. He rules us with a rod of aluminum."

"Don't you mean iron?"

"Iron rusts, and my uncle is indestructible! Iron also is heavy, and my uncle has a light touch. He gets what he wants through humor and suggestion. Not like Nico," he added. "He has a temper like a bull!"

"Is he the same age as you?"

"A few years older. But much older in his outlook. That's because he was brought up by my uncle."

"You mean he didn't go to school?"

"Most of the time he had tutors."

"Being groomed for his role of Emperor," she murmured.

"Emperor wouldn't be so bad," Leon replied. "But sometimes Nico thinks he's God!"

As if he found the subject of his cousin disagreeable, he started to talk about horse racing, displaying an astonishing knowledge of a sport about which Alex knew little and cared even less. Surreptitiously she glanced at her watch. Midnight. It was time to go.

"And now we'll go dancing," he announced. "It will give me a chance to hold you in my arms."

It was a remark she had expected from him, and she stifled her boredom. "I'm sure you say that to all the girls you know."

"But with you I mean it."

"I'm sure you've said that too!"

"Are you jealous?"

She laughed. "Not in the least."

"I *want* you to be jealous of me, Alex. I want you to think of me and wonder where I am when I'm not with you. I want to be in your mind last thing at night and first thing in the morning."

"I'll think of you each time I brush my teeth!"

"You're making fun of me," he reproached.

"You can't expect me to take you seriously?"

"You should. I mean everything I say." He pushed back his chair. "Come on. I know an amusing little disco farther along the coast. We can—"

"It's too late for me to go dancing." She was suddenly anxious to end the evening. "As it is, I won't be home till one. And it's baking day tomorrow, which means we start cooking at seven o'clock."

"Close down for a few days."

"That's impossible."

"Why? If it's a question of money I—"

"Please!" Her voice was tight with anger, and he was quick to notice it.

"Forgive me, Alex, I do not mean to make it sound as if I'm buying your time. But now I've found you, I want to be with you every moment I can."

"I'm not going anywhere else," she said lightly. "But don't *you* work?"

"When I'm in Paris. At the moment I'm on holiday. A busman's holiday," he added. "Nico doesn't believe in anyone having a complete rest."

"You didn't seem to be working hard today!"

"Because Nico was in Marseilles." They had reached the car, and he helped her in. "Are you sure you want to go home so early?" At her nod, he sighed. "Very well, home it is."

"I suppose you're staying on the coast?" she said as she settled back in her seat. "I'm sorry to give you such a long drive."

"I like driving." He spurted forward and then slowed down. "Our villa is at Cap Ferrat."

She noticed his use of the word "our" and wondered if he meant his own family or that of his uncle. Instinctively she felt it was the latter. Uncle and cousin sounded an odd pair, to say the least: feudal lord and heir apparent, both living in a world where what they said was law.

"If Nico is still in Marseilles tomorrow," Leon continued, "I will come and see you in the afternoon. Otherwise it will be the same time as tonight." He lifted one hand from the wheel and touched her cheek. "We are going to have fun, Alex. Fun and a lot of happiness." He paused, as though waiting for her to say something. When she remained silent, he spoke again. "I hope you don't keep your café open on a Sunday?"

"Not at the moment."

"Good. At least we can be together one whole day."

"I wouldn't want to leave my godmother alone for an entire day."

"Then we will take her out to lunch. And afterwards I will send her back in the car, and we can spend the rest of the day alone."

"You may change your mind by Sunday. It's a long way off."

"Only four days."

"You might get bored with me by then."

"I will not answer such a remark. I prefer to let my actions speak for me."

For the next three weeks, Leon's actions spoke of devotion and persistence. He was a constant visitor to the cottage and, as Alex got to know him better, she grew to like him more. It was true he lived on the surface of life, but it kept him lighthearted and made him an acceptable companion with whom to while away some of her leisure.

"Don't you ever do any work?" she asked one Sunday when he suggested they spend the whole of the next day together.

"Of course I do. But Nico and my uncle are in New York for a few weeks, and when the cats are away, the mouse plays!"

"You play all the time," she scoffed.

"That shows how little you know me." He caught her hand and drew it to his lips. They were lunching at the Colombe d'Or, a beautiful hotel in the picturesque village of St.-Paul-de-Vence. Their table was on the terrace, and below them silver-green olive trees rustled their leaves like so many dancing skirts.

"You don't know me at all," he repeated, "and I must rectify it at once."

"You're doing your best," she smiled. "You've seen me nearly every day since we met."

"I wish I could see you every night." His voice lowered. "All night." Her lack of response did not deter him. "Don't you care about me a little?"

"A little," she agreed.

"I want to make it more than a little. I love you, Alex."

"You don't know me."

"How can you say that? I've seen you constantly for three weeks."

It was impossible for her to explain that knowing someone did not depend on the length of time or the frequency one saw them. One could know and love someone after meeting them a couple of times; equally, one could see a person for months and never know them at all. But she could not say this to Leon without hurting him.

"Perhaps you know *me*," she demurred, "but I don't know *you*."

"We can easily remedy that. Come away with me for a holiday. We can go to Corsica or Sardinia—or anywhere else you like."

"I'd rather go to the cottage instead," she replied, looking at her watch. "I told Eleanor I'd be home for tea."

Disgruntled, he paid the bill and led her to the car. "You still haven't answered my question," he said as they drove off. "Will you come away with me?"

"No."

"Why not?"

"I'm old-fashioned," she said dryly. "I believe one should love a man before one sleeps with him."

"I see." He hesitated, then said: "Have you ever been in love?"

"I've never slept with anyone," she replied, "so that should answer your question!"

"What have you done with your life? It's incredible that you've never had a love affair." He flung her a beseeching look. "Don't I mean anything to you?"

"What do I mean to *you*?" she prevaricated. "A fortnight in Sardinia?"

"Is that why you said no?" He drew the car to a stop. "You think I only want a holiday affair?" He slid across the seat toward her. "I want to marry you, Alex. I thought you knew that." Her look of astonishment made him chuckle, and he put his arms around her. "You shouldn't be so quick to judge me, my angel."

Before she could say anything, he took possession of her mouth. His lips were hard and demanding, and for a moment she suffered his touch. But as his teeth pressed upon her lips, she made herself go limp in his arms. Seeing it as surrender, his grip relaxed, and instantly she pulled away from him and slid to the far corner of the front seat.

"What's wrong?" he asked. "Are you still angry with me?"

"No. I was never that. I'm used to being propositioned. It's one of the problems a single girl learns to contend with."

"Then why won't you kiss me?"

"I don't love you, Leon."

He folded his arms and looked at her. He was in no way put out by her statement, and his next words told her why.

"You are afraid to love, Alex. For all your fine talk, you're a scared girl." His eyes glinted. "I never thought it possible to meet someone who still had my mother's morality—but I have! And I'm delighted."

Alex looked away from him. She almost told him that morality didn't come into it and then decided that perhaps it did. Perhaps she demanded too much from a man. Perhaps her deep belief that one day Prince Charming would appear had kept her emotionally isolated. Yet what would happen if her ideal remained a hope that never materialized? Would she be able to accept second best? It was something she must start to consider. But not now; and definitely not Leon.

"*I* am the man you are looking for," he stated. "Marry me, Alex."

"Be your wife?" She stared at him. "You can't be serious."

"Do you think I propose to a girl as a joke?"

"Of course not." She was contrite not wishing to upset his easily ruffled equilibrium. "It wouldn't work, Leon. We're too different."

"We're not. We can have a wonderful life together. Please, Alex, listen to me. There are so many things we can do, so much I can give you."

"I don't love you," she reiterated. "I'm terribly flattered by your proposal, but I can't accept it. It wouldn't be fair to you."

"If *I'm* willing—"

"No Leon, I can't."

Silently he switched on the engine. Alex knew he had not accepted her refusal, and for the first time she wondered if she were foolhardy for saying no. He was good-looking, obviously rich, and would make an amenable husband. She tried to think of him as a lover and failed to feel any thrill at the prospect. That, more than anything else, told her she had made the right decision.

The village clock was chiming four as Leon parked the car in the lane beside the cottage and walked with her up the crumbling stone steps to the front door.

"One bad storm and the terrace wall will collapse," he commented as a shower of loose stones moved under his feet.

"We've asked a mason to fix it, but once the season begins, it's impossible to get things done. Everyone rushes down to work in the hotels."

"I'll send along one of our own men."

"Do you own a building company too?"

"Nico permanently employs a couple of men at the villa," he replied. "He's always improving things. I tell him that one day he'll have nothing more to improve and will cut his throat from frustration!"

"Or buy another villa," she smiled and entered the cottage.

Eleanor was in the kitchen making tea and looked round as Alex and Leon came in. "I baked you some scones," she said, proffering a plateful.

"My favorite food," Leon exclaimed and munched one with gusto.

"I'm glad you like an English tea," Eleanor said, leading the way on to the terrace.

"I like an English girl, too. I have asked your god-daughter to be my wife."

Eleanor flung Alex a look of amazement, which changed to quickly disguised relief as Alex said:

"Leon also forgot to tell you I refused his proposal."

"I'm not going to take no for an answer," he intervened. "I will make you change your mind." He moved to the steps. "I will leave the two of you to talk together and will call for you again at eight o'clock."

"Can't we leave it for another night?" she suggested.

"I have made plans," he said firmly. "Be ready for me."

He strode away across the lawn and Eleanor raised her brows. "Are you sure you don't want to marry him? He has a lot to offer."

"I'd love what he has to offer," Alex confessed, "but unfortunately *he* comes with it!"

"Then you'd better make it clear to him that you meant what you said. Otherwise he'll keep pestering you. He's a young man who's always had his own way, and he won't like being thwarted."

"I'll tell him tonight," Alex promised. "And I won't mince my words."

But her avowal to do so was negated by Leon's unexpected mood of depression, which, she learned over dinner, was due to a row he had had with his cousin.

"I thought he was in New York," she said in surprise.

"He came back this afternoon. Apparently my mother telephoned him and asked him to return."

Alex waited for him to explain why and, when he didn't, searched for something to say.

"I didn't realize your mother lived here."

"She has an apartment in Menton." He scowled. "It's the right place for her to live: retired old colonels and spinsters with their cats. She's so old-fashioned, you wouldn't think she lived in the twentieth century."

"Earlier today you were delighted that *I* was equally old-fashioned." Alex tried to inject some humor into the scene, but Leon was not to be amused.

"She still looks upon me as a child," he muttered.

"Parents have a habit of doing that," Alex placated.

"Well, I refuse to pander to it. I have my own life to live, and I won't let her dictate to me."

"I can't imagine *anyone* dictating to you," Alex lied, and she was rewarded by the gratified look he gave her. Leon might appear headstrong and impulsive, but he was Greek and family-conscious; and this, she was sure, meant complying with his family's wishes.

"Let's get out of here," he said abruptly. "I want to be alone with you."

She followed him, nervously thinking of the scene that lay ahead of her. Leon was spoiled and would be angry when she said she did not want to see him any more. But she had to tell him: for his own peace of mind as well as hers. She glanced at his profile and wondered why his dark good looks failed to arouse her. Perhaps she was incapable of falling in love? It was a new thought and a scaring one, and she was still pondering on it when Leon stopped the car in a parking place and pulled her firmly but inexorably into his arms.

"I love you," he muttered. "I won't let anyone part us."

His head lowered to hers, but she twisted away and,

anxious to keep him talking, pretended a deep interest in what he was saying.

"Who wants to part us, Leon?"

"Nico. But only because of my mother."

"Is that why he flew back? Because you're going out with *me*?"

"Yes."

Many things became clear in Alex's mind. The Panos family was afraid that one of its members would marry a non-Greek! That was why the heir apparent had flown posthaste from New York. But how could the great Nico put a brake on Leon's behavior? Without any difficulty, she knew the answer. Leon worked for his cousin and would be expected to toe the family line. If he didn't, he'd be out of a magnificently paid job.

"If your family objects to me," she murmured, "it would be better if we stopped seeing each other."

"Do you think that will stop me from loving you?"

"It might."

"You are as stupid as Nico!" he said angrily. "Don't you believe I know my own mind? Do you think me a child who will want a new toy every week to play with?"

Once more he tried to take her in his arms, but she firmly held him at bay. "No, Leon. I don't want you to make love to me. I haven't changed my mind since this afternoon."

For a brief instant she had the impression he was going to ignore what she said, and she looked at him fearlessly, sensing this was the only way of warding him off.

"Very well," he muttered and turned back to the wheel.

The journey to Cabray was a silent one save for the sound of tires screeching on the tarmac. Alex clenched her hands on her lap and kept her mouth shut, knowing the futility of telling him to drive slowly. One good thing about such speed was that she'd be home earlier than usual. The humorous thought eased her tension, allowing her body to move with the swing of the car instead of fighting it.

Only as they reached the lane leading to the cottage did Leon slow down, and, face still dark with temper, he stopped the car outside the tumbledown gates.

"Don't bother seeing me to the door," she murmured and jumped out before he could prevent her.

She heard him call her name, but she pretended she hadn't and began to run across the grass. Behind her the engine throbbed into life again and she drew a breath of relief. If only he would go and never come back!

Any doubts she had had about refusing to marry him had gone forever. She didn't love him and she never would. It was a pity she couldn't tell his mother so. The poor woman was worrying for nothing!

Alex slowed her pace and paused to catch her breath. Even telling Mrs. Panos might not convince her. It would take a very special mother to believe that an out-of-work actress had no intention of marrying her rich and handsome son.

Chapter Four

The knowledge that Leon's family considered her enough of a threat for his cousin to return from New York made Alex realize Leon was serious in his desire to marry her. He was used to girls running after him because of the Panos fortune; to meet one who didn't had fired his ardor. Obviously the autocratic Nico did not believe she was serious in her refusal of Leon; otherwise he would not have responded so quickly to his aunt's call. What a surprise he would have when Leon told him there was one girl who was not bowled over by dreams of wealth.

The knowledge that the Panos family had misjudged her made her even more determined to stop seeing Leon, much as she enjoyed the luxurious places to which he took her.

"He'll still pester you," Eleanor said, reiterating

51

what she had already stated. "Your only way of es-
caping him is to return to England. Anyway, it's time
you resumed your career. I've already asked Monsieur
Brun if he knows anyone who can help me part-time,
and he said his wife would inquire."

"So you declare me redundant!"

"For your own good."

"I'll write to Sherry today," Alex promised, "and
tell her I'm coming home. If I—" She stopped as a
small Moped chugged to a halt at the bottom of the
terrace steps. The young boy on the machine was
holding up a telegram.

"Ma'm'selle Godfrey?" he enquired.

Alex nodded and hurried down to get it. What a
wonderful coincidence if it was Sherry telling her there
was a job waiting for her. She tore open the envelope,
her excitement waning as she read it.

"It's from Leon," she explained, returning to the
terrace. "He's had to go to Greece unexpectedly and
will be there for several weeks."

Eleanor snorted. "That sounds like something his
cousin dreamed up in order to get him out of your
grasping clutches! I bet Nicolas Panos thinks he's done
you one in the eye by sending Leon away."

Alex chuckled. "How disappointed he'd be if he
knew he'd done exactly what I wanted! It means I
can stay on here without any problems."

"I'm not sure you should. Hibernating is fine for
an old woman like me, but—"

"Stuff and nonsense!" Alex rejoined. "A few more
weeks' sunshine is just what I need."

Eleanor's reply was forestalled by the arrival of
some customers. The fame of their café had spread

in the intervening weeks, and many tourists from other villages came to sample the homemade baking.

"If we get any busier, we'll have to put up extra tables," Alex murmured, dabbing perspiration from her forehead during a momentary lull in serving coffee.

"Over my dead body!" Eleanor said instantly. "More customers mean more cooking."

"And more money too."

"No! I refuse to wear myself out—or you, either— just to put a few more francs into the bank."

Alex was thinking of this as she left the kitchen with a laden tray. Rounding the side of the terrace she immediately noticed the man at the corner table and, with a certainty that came from intuition rather than knowledge, knew it was Nicolas Panos.

Inwardly seething but outwardly calm, she approached him. That he had come to see her for himself was obvious; the only question that remained was for what purpose?

"Good morning," she said brightly and waited for him to introduce himself.

Instead, he nodded unsmilingly and asked for a black coffee. She went to fetch it, wondering if she had been wrong in her guess as to who he was. His accent wasn't French, but it was lighter than Leon's, and he could be Italian or even from Eastern Europe.

"Of course it's Leon's cousin," Eleanor said, peeping quickly through the living room window when Alex told her of her suspicions. "He looks exactly like his photographs. The French papers are always writing about him," she added.

"Then why didn't he introduce himself?"

"Because he wants to look you over and find out what sort of girl you are."

"Before he welcomes me into the family?" Alex asked drily.

"Before he decides how much it will cost him to buy you off!"

"You don't mean. . . . " Alex struggled for words. "You aren't suggesting he. . . . *Oh no!*"

"Oh yes," Eleanor replied. "The Panos family are bound to be concerned when one of their men wants to marry an unknown girl—and an actress to boot!"

"If he says one wrong word to me," Alex said crisply, "I'll hit him over the head with his coffeepot!"

"Why don't you introduce yourself when you serve him? That should take the wind out of his sails."

"He might think I was trying to suck up to him. I wouldn't dream of treating him as anything other than a customer."

"Then try and control your temper when he reaches for his checkbook."

"He wouldn't dare!"

"Maybe not. He could have come here simply to see if he likes you. And if he does—"

"He'll give Leon permission to marry me!" Alex tossed her head, and her gleaming gold hair, caught back from her face by a black velvet ribbon, swung magnificently behind her. "It will give me great satisfaction to tell him I've no intention of marrying his eligible cousin."

"I bet *that* will surprise him."

"But I'll bide my time before I do," Alex continued. "First of all, I'll find out how much he's willing to pay to buy me off. Then I'll tell him exactly what he can do with his money!"

Setting the coffeepot on the tray, she marched out. The subject of their conversation was staring at the garden, and she was able to study him without being observed. Seen in profile, he was totally unlike Leon. His features were more aquiline, with a large, well-defined nose, a firm chin, and a tightly set mouth with beautifully shaped but thin lips. Because she could see only his profile, she could not read his expression, and even when he turned to watch her set his coffee and cup down in front of him, his lids were lowered over his eyes, making it impossible for her to see their color or expression. He was as dark-skinned as his cousin and had the same jet-black hair, but whereas Leon's was shiny with brilliantine to keep out the curl, this man's was thick and straight as a lion's mane and brushed back from a high forehead to fall down the back of his head, almost to the collar of his open-necked, cream silk sweater.

"If you change your mind and would like some scones," she said with commendable calmness, "please let me know."

"I never eat between meals."

His voice was as commanding as his appearance, being resonant and deep. It was the deepness that gave it a false quality of warmth, for there was none of that in his eyes, which were now staring at her intently. They were dark eyes—as she had expected them to be—but with none of Leon's spaniellike devotion. These eyes were cold and critical.

"It's unusual to find a café in a place like Cabray," he commented. "How long has it been open?"

"Since the beginning of the season." Deliberately, she said no more and waited for him to speak again.

"Don't you find living here rather quiet? A beautiful young girl like you would do better on the coast."

"Do better?" she questioned coldly.

"Fun and excitement."

"I have no wish for fun and excitement."

She was finding it difficult to control her temper and was able to do so only by reminding herself of the pleasure in store for her when she finally gave this man his comeuppance.

"I find that hard to believe." He challenged her statement. "You don't look the type to be happy among the peasants."

"I find them less obnoxious than the Riviera play-boys!"

For a split second, he was taken by surprise. "You speak as if you know them."

"I've read about them," she said laconically and moved away to serve another table.

All the while she was conscious of him watching her and was reminded of the first time Leon had come here. How long ago it seemed, yet it was barely a month. For an instant, she toyed with the idea of going up to this man and telling him he had no need to worry that his cousin had been snared by a gold digger.

She took a step toward the table, and simultaneously he turned from looking at the view and stared at her. The contempt in his eyes was so apparent that anger choked her. How dare he prejudge her in this high-handed way? If he was so sure she was out for what she could get, then it would serve him right to live

with his fears a bit longer. She thought of Leon wing-
ing his way to Athens—forced to leave France because
this was the only way his family could part him from
her—and wished with all her heart that she loved him
enough to marry him. What a cat that would have set
among the canaries!

Nicolas Panos raised his hand in her direction, and
she came over to him with the bill. Without glancing
at it, he placed a ten franc note on the table and stood
up to walk away. Standing, she found him far taller
than she had expected: all of six feet with shoulders
to match and a lithe way of walking that indicated
extreme physical fitness. He might work and play hard,
as Leon had said, but there were no marks of dissipa-
tion on his face. Picking up the ten franc note, she
hurried down the steps after him.

"You've forgotten your change, Monsieur."

"I wasn't expecting any, Ma'm'selle."

"We're content to make a fair profit; we don't wish
for an exorbitant one."

He pocketed the change she handed to him. "I
never knew anyone to turn down a bigger profit. You
aren't a good businesswoman."

"We prefer to remain happy amateurs."

"A characteristic of the English," he said drily.
"They enjoy being amateurs. It makes the necessity of
winning less onerous!"

"But we generally do win," she reminded him.

"You did in the past," he corrected and, nodding
farewell, walked away from her.

Furious with his parting comment, she retreated to
the terrace, though it was not until later in the day,
when she had more leisure, that she went over her

conversation with him and wished she had made a
better show of herself. Her remarks had been sharp,
but he had regarded them as mere pinpricks. If only
she could have annihilated him with her sarcasm or
bowled him over with her charm. Instead, she had
made herself look irritable and childish.

"Who's winning?" Eleanor asked.

"Winning what?"

"The battle you're having with yourself. It *is* with
yourself and not Nicolas Panos, isn't it?"

"Yes." Briefly Alex told her godmother of her
thoughts. "What do you think he'll do now?" she
concluded.

"It depends whether he still considers you unsuitable. If he doesn't, he'll probably wait for Leon to
introduce you to him officially."

"I've no intention of meeting Leon's family. I am
not going to marry him." Alex frowned. "But if
Nicolas Panos *didn't* like me, do you think he'd still
come back and try to buy me off?"

"Do you think a girl *can* be bought off? I mean, if
someone were really after Leon because of his money,
surely whatever the family offered as an inducement
would be far less than she could get if she became his
wife?"

"*If* she became his wife," Eleanor agreed. "But she'd
be taking a chance—with the odds stacked against
her. Leon might propose marriage, but he could still
stipulate an agreement about divorce. It's the sort of
thing these rich Greeks do."

"How awful to consider money the be-all of your
existence."

"It has its compensations!" There was a pause. "What will you do if Nicolas Panos comes back?"

"Charm him," Alex said promptly.

"You want *two* Greek beaux to your string?"

Alex pursed her lips. Her answer to her godmother's question had been flippant, but now she considered it seriously. The idea had much to commend it, and, the more she thought of it, the more attractive it became. It would be amusing—to say the least—to bring a man like Nicolas Panos to heel.

"Still," Eleanor continued, "he might think you're just the girl to make Leon happy. In which case he won't come back at all."

In this, Eleanor was proved wrong, for the Greek arrived next afternoon and, taking the same corner table, drank several cups of black coffee while he smoked a long and expensive cigar. Today he wore a blue silk sweater with slacks of a darker hue. The clothes intensified his dark, strong looks and drew attention to the supple lines of his body. He could not be more than thirty-two or three, yet he had an air of authority that gave weight to his years. He was not a man to be gainsaid, Alex mused, but to be obeyed implicitly.

As she went about her duties, she knew he was watching her, but this time when she looked up and met his eyes, there was less of a mocking expression in them, and, when she gave him the bill, he asked her if she would join him for a drink. She longed to tell him this was the way she had met Leon, but since she was not supposed to know who he was, she smiled and shook her head.

"I'm too busy to sit down with you. There are several tables still waiting to be served."

"I'm in no hurry. I can wait until things slacken off."

"That won't be until we close."

"When is that?"

"At five o'clock."

"Isn't that rather early?"

"Not for us. By five o'clock, my godmother and I are exhausted."

"Why do you do it, then? Is having money so important to you?"

"We have no ambition to own the world, Mr.—" Only with luck did she prevent herself from saying his name, and, realizing she was dangerously close to showing her real feelings, she walked away.

She was kept busy until shortly before five, when, seeing three customers coming through the gate, she leaned the chairs on the tables to signify the café was closed. But Nicolas Panos remained at his table and made no move to go.

"We are closed, Monsieur," she said stiffly.

"No more coffee?"

"We are no longer open to customers."

"A cup of coffee for an acquaintance, then? I know I dare not call myself a friend!"

He was deliberately teasing her, and it in no way appeased her anger.

"If you are in desperate need of more coffee," she said stiffly, "I will bring you a cup."

"Forget it." He stood up but remained where he was. The only way Alex could reach the kitchen was to push past him or make a detour, and she was debating what to do when Eleanor came on to the terrace, yawning and stretching her arms high.

"Sorry," she apologized as she saw them. "I thought everyone had gone."

"Are you the excellent cook responsible for the food and delicious cakes?" the Greek asked.

"Yes. I'm glad you enjoyed them."

"This customer hasn't tasted them," Alex said with precision. "He's only guessing."

"Having watched everyone eating around me," he said smoothly, "no guesswork was required!"

Eleanor laughed. "Perhaps I can persuade you to try something for yourself? I've just made some fresh coffee for Alex and myself, and if you would like to join us. . . . "

"I'd be delighted." He sprang forward and held out a chair for Eleanor, leaving Alex to go to the kitchen and set the tray.

She did so irritably and was in the act of picking it up when two sinewy arms appeared on either side of her and took hold of it, imprisoning her within their circle. Quickly she turned, finding Nicolas Panos so close that her hair brushed his cheek. At once he stepped back though he still kept hold of the tray.

"It's too heavy for you," he stated and carried it out.

"I'm used to carrying trays," she protested, following him.

"So I've noticed. You went backwards and forwards to the kitchen fifty-one times this afternoon."

She was taken aback to know he had counted. "Exercise is good for the figure."

"Yours does not need any improvement."

They were on the terrace, and he set the tray down in front of Eleanor and accepted the coffee she poured for him.

"Excellent," he murmured as he sipped it. "I am extremely fond of coffee."

"Most Continentals are," Eleanor said.

His eyebrows, black as his hair, drew together. "I am Greek!"

"Isn't that Continental?"

"No. Greeks have a toughness and strength that is lacking in the Latin." He looked down at his cup and said abruptly, "My name is Nicolas Panos."

There was a second of silence, and Eleanor stared at Alex, who returned the look with one of blankness.

"Leon's cousin?" the older said with such surprise that Alex, hearing her, decided her godmother would have done well on the stage.

"You know my cousin?" the man answered, his surprise so much like Eleanor's that Alex was forced to award him full marks for acting, too.

"But of course," Eleanor gushed. "Leon was a frequent visitor here. He loved my scones." She held out the plate to Alex, winking at her surreptitiously as she did so.

Alex took a scone and pretended to be unaware of the dark eyes that were watching her. When the silence had gone on for what seemed an interminable length of time, the man broke it by speaking directly to her.

"You know my cousin, too?"

"Yes."

"He has gone to Greece."

"I know. He wrote and told me. It was a sudden departure."

"The unexpected frequently happens in business. He may be away a long time."

She shrugged, leaving him to make what he liked of this gesture. When was he going to ask her how much she wanted to stay out of Leon's life, she wondered.

"Will you?" he asked.

Blankly she stared at him. "I'm sorry, I didn't hear what you said."

"I asked if you were free to have dinner with me tonight."

For an instant she was motionless, then she shook her head. "I'm afraid not. It's been a long day, and I'm tired."

The lids half lowered over the intense dark eyes, giving a shuttered look to his face that made his expression hard to judge.

"No longer than your other working days."

Though unspoken, the words "When you were not too tired to see Leon" were clearly in the air.

"I'm sorry," she said.

"Perhaps you will feel less tired another night?"

"Perhaps." She rose and moved towards the kitchen. "If you will excuse me, Mr. Panos, I have things to do."

She was by the sink, washing the last of the crockery, when she heard the throaty roar of an engine in the lane and knew he was leaving. Almost at once, Eleanor came in, relaxed and amused.

"I don't think the poor man has ever been turned

down by a girl before. I thought he was going to faint from shock!"

"Serve him right if he had!"

"You can't dislike him that much. I thought he was rather charming."

"Charming! When he came sneaking in here to spy on me? If you call that charming . . . . " Crossly Alex rattled the cups and saucers in the soapy water.

"You can't blame him for what he's doing," Eleanor said in a more serious tone. "After all, you don't know the kind of girls Leon took out before he met you. They could well have been the sort to worry his family."

"So what?"

"So Mr. Panos came to see what *you* were like."

"And, now he's found out, what does he intend doing? Ask me to have dinner with him to vet my manners?"

"I think he asked you because he likes you."

"Likes me!" Alex was scornful. "You can't be that naïve. It's all part of the softening-up process before he tries to buy me off."

"Perhaps he isn't going to. He could have asked you because he wants to know you better."

"Really!" Alex was beyond words. "Let's stop talking about him, shall we? He's gone, and with any luck we won't be seeing him again."

"You can't believe that. He came here for a reason, and he won't disappear from your life until he's done what he set out to do—whatever that may be!"

"If he comes back and starts talking to me about Leon, I'll make it quite clear we're only friends. I'm fed up with all this subterfuge."

"You'll never get a Greek to believe a man and a woman can be friends and nothing more," Eleanor replied. "And if all Greek men are like Nicolas Panos, I can understand why!"

Chapter
Five

Four days passed without Nicolas
returning to the cottage, and Alex assumed he was
going to let matters rest while his cousin was in Greece.
Unlike Eleanor, she did not believe he would ever
approve of a mixed marriage. Greek families liked to
keep their fortunes among themselves and did not believe that marrying a foreigner and bringing new blood
into the line would increase their strength. On the
contrary, they believed their strength came from their
very Greekness. Because of this, she was sure that
even if Nicolas Panos had liked her, he would never
agree to her marrying his cousin.

"But it's all academic," she muttered out loud one
morning, when she again found herself thinking of the
Panos family. "I could never marry a Greek, anyway.

They treat their women like second-class citizens and confine them to the kitchen or the bed!"

If Nicolas Panos came back, she would tell him so in no uncertain terms. An image of him came clearly to her mind—far clearer than her image of Leon. It was not surprising, of course, for he had a much stronger personality. No matter in what company he was, he would never go unnoticed. It had nothing to do with his wealth or power; rather it came from the inner strength and tenacity of the man, which she had sensed on the first occasion she had seen him.

It was a pity her pride had prevented her from accepting his invitation to dinner, for it would have been interesting to try and find out what he was like beneath the controlled veneer. She had read a long article written about him in a French magazine that Eleanor had unearthed for her only the night before. In it, his views on many things had been assessed, not from direct quotations—since he never gave interviews —but from the rare speeches he had made and the things he had done.

"I'd discount most of what you read about him," Eleanor warned. "I'm sure a lot of it is made up."

Though she conceded this, Alex nonetheless felt that several of the comments about him were justified: one of them being his attitude to women, which was highly suspicious, to say the least. Because of this, he mixed only with rich and cosseted ones, and, in the many pictures that had graced the article, they all looked like highly bred racehorses, their hair and skin glossy from pampered grooming, their eyes shining with the blinkered innocence of eyes that had seen no poverty or pain.

What opportunity did a man in his position have of meeting an ordinary girl, and, if he did, how could he be sure she would remain ordinary once she was given the chance of sharing his wealth? The power of the Panoses was enough to turn anyone's head, and it was not to be wondered at that he preferred to choose his girlfriends from the wealthy few whom he knew would not admire him for his money alone.

She was so engrossed with her thoughts that she did not notice anyone crossing the grass until she heard steps on the terrace and, turning, saw the tall figure of the man she was thinking about.

As always he looked as if he had been groomed by a valet, and she felt a flicker of irritation that he should take so much trouble with his appearance. He was dressed for a day on one of the expensive beaches along the Côte d'Azur rather than for a drive into the less fashionable region of Haute-Provence. Hastily she dismissed the thought as uncharitable. He was the type of man who would be well groomed no matter what he wore or where he went. To expect him not to wear the best was merely to be carping.

"I'm glad to find you taking it easy," he said by way of greeting.

"We aren't open for another half hour," she explained, "but if you'd like some coffee, I'll—"

"I haven't come for the coffee. I came to see you. I hope you will change your mind about having dinner with me. Your refusal the other day was only an excuse."

She remained silent, and he drew a chair forward and sat astride it, resting his strong arms along the back.

"Will you?" he asked.

"Will I what?"

"Change your mind and accept my invitation?"

"No."

His brows contracted. "Is it because I'm Leon's cousin? Are you worried that he will object?"

"I have given no man the right to object to what I do," she retorted.

He gave a slight smile which lightened the depths of his dark eyes. "An emancipated woman, I see."

"Let's not start that argument," she said coldly.

"There will be no argument. I am all for women taking their rightful place in society. I believe the correct expression is 'doing their own thing.'"

The slang remark sounded strange in his deep, accented voice, and she gave an involuntary smile.

"That's good," he said. "It's the first time you've smiled at something I've said."

"It's the first time you've said something to amuse me!"

He drew a sharp breath, as if not sure how to take her remark. But when he spoke, his voice was still friendly. "If you will have dinner with me, I'll have a chance of amusing you even more."

It seemed childish to keep refusing him. Besides, he obviously intended to get her alone sooner or later. It was on the tip of her tongue to tell him he had no need to waste his valuable time on her since she had no intention of marrying his cousin, but she was stopped by an impulse she could not define. Perhaps it stemmed from a curiosity to see what he was like when he set out to be entertaining—as he undoubtedly would be if his intention was to soften her up before approaching the subject of Leon.

"I am free tonight, Mr. Panos."

If he was surprised by her *volte-face*, he hid it well. "What time would you like me to collect you?"

"What time is best for you?" she replied.

"You are the one who is working at the moment. I wasn't sure if you wanted to have a rest before going out."

Surprised by his thoughtfulness, she shook her head. "I'll be ready any time after seven."

"Then I will call for you at seven-thirty. That should give us time for a leisurely dinner, and I can bring you back before midnight."

"Is that when your car turns into a pumpkin?"

He frowned, and she knew he had not understood the allusion. "I was talking about Cinderella," she explained.

"Ah." He smiled and shook his head. "No pumpkin, Miss Godfrey, merely my desire not to keep you out too late and rob your cheeks of their bloom."

Again his thoughtfulness surprised her, though the flowery phrases brought Leon to mind. But watching the man in front of her, she had the impression he meant what he said. How disconcerting to meet someone who talked like an English translation of the *Illiad*!

"Until this evening," he said and moved down the steps.

"Did you drive up here just to ask me out?" she called, and he stopped and turned.

He was several steps below her, and she was able to look down on him. His dark hair was not as straight as she had imagined, for at the back it had a slight tendency to curl.

"It was either that or send a carrier pigeon!" he replied. "Do you not find it inconvenient to be without a telephone?"

"We'd find it more inconvenient if we had to pay the bills! Do you know how much French telephones cost?"

"I should. I have four different lines at the villa! Until seven-thirty," he repeated and went on his way.

The only comment Eleanor made when she learned Alex was going out with Nicolas Panos was to implore her not to lose her temper when he broached the subject of Leon's proposal.

"After all," she went on, "in his position you might do exactly the same."

"I'd never think that my money gave me the right to control what others do."

"But if your money could protect them? That's what Nicolas is doing. Try to see it from that point of view."

"If he still thinks that way about me," Alex said crisply, "then he's a lousy judge of character."

"Or very cynical. In which case one should pity him."

"Very well," Alex answered swiftly. "I'll pity him. He'll be pitying himself by the time I've told him what I think of him!"

A streak of perversity made her put on the same cream pleated dress she had worn for her first evening with Leon. It suited her even more now than it had done before, for her skin was more deeply tanned, and that enhanced the golden blonde of her hair. Tonight she wore it loose around her shoulders, and she was fiercely glad she looked beautiful.

She peered at herself in the mirror, wishing it had more size and less antiquity. But even in its small surface she could not find fault with her clear skin and wide-apart eyes fringed by lashes so long and dark that most people thought them false. Her eyes themselves were shining with a strange expectancy, and, as always, their color reflected her mood: dark grey when she was unhappy; silver-grey when she was excited. Now they gleamed like silver, and she turned away from the mirror and went downstairs.

Expecting Nicolas Panos to be on time, she was surprised when seven-thirty came and went without his arrival. Did he intend to stand her up? Was this his way of showing her how unimportant she was? Somehow she could not believe it, though when another half hour had gone by, her doubts became a certainty.

"I'm sure he has a reason for being late," Eleanor said, "and he has no way of letting you know."

"If he *does* come, then he is being late deliberately."

"He wouldn't be so petty." The grey head tilted. "I think I can hear his car."

Alex heard it, too, but made no move to go to the door until there was the rap of knuckles on the wood. Only then did she open it. It was dark outside, and the light from the hall shone full upon the Greek's face, making his skin the color of mahogany.

"Forgive me for being late, but I had a call from New York as I was on the point of leaving."

"The penance of power," she said sarcastically.

"Tonight was the first time I thought of it as a penance. Knowing you were waiting for me made me impatient."

She was surprised not so much by the compliment—for she still felt his flowery address to be part of his plan to disarm her—but by the fact that he did not mind making it in front of her godmother. But then, he and Leon were cousins, and neither of them had the reticence an Englishman would have shown in a similar situation.

"Would you like a drink?" she asked ungraciously.

"Not unless you would."

She shook her head and a few moments later was sitting beside him as they headed towards the coast. Like Leon, he was a fast driver, but here the similarity ended, for his speed was controlled, and he did not hug the center of the road but kept well to the side, braking carefully whenever they came to an intersection. The car was also much smaller than she had expected, and though she stared round it carefully, she could not see a name or fitting she recognized.

"Do you like it?" he asked, sensing her curiosity.

"It goes," she said nonchalantly.

"I had it designed for me."

"Naturally."

He gave an exclamation. "Are you always so rude to your escorts?"

"If I go out under duress."

"I thought you wanted to come out with me?"

She shrugged. "I knew that until I did, you wouldn't give me any peace!"

"Are you suggesting that once I've taken you out, I won't want to repeat the experience?"

"There won't be any need. After all, you're only—"
She stopped, angry with herself for having said so
much.

"Well?" he asked, glancing at her before turning
his attention back to the road. "Aren't you going to
finish the sentence?"

"Is it necessary?"

"Most definitely." He slowed the car and pulled
into the side of the road. Resting his hands on the
wheel, he turned 'round to look at her. "Finish it,
please."

She clenched her hands but faced him bravely.
"You only asked me out in order to warn me off Leon!"

"I see." His voice was mild, though the rest of his
words were sharp. "So you think I intend to seduce
you with food and wine before I try to buy you off?"

She had not expected such bluntness but was glad
of it, for now all pretence had gone. "Isn't it true? At
least thank me for saving you the dinner! You can
make your offer now and then take me home."

He leaned towards her so swiftly that she thought
he was going to hit her. But all he did was to make
sure her door was secure before he set the car in
motion again, driving with a controlled fury that indicated his temper far more than anything he could
have said.

She sat beside him in silence as the miles were con-
sumed. It was too dark for her to see where they were
going, and the lights of the coast were nowhere in
evidence. They could be miles in the heart of Provence
for all she knew, as indeed they were, she discovered,
when his headlamps picked out a signpost, and she
saw the name Lejure.

A mile farther on, he stopped outside a stone house set back from the road in its own garden. Parking the car within the sound of a rushing stream, he escorted her down a flagstoned path into a room that housed no more than six tables.

Four of them were already occupied, though none of the diners looked up at their entry. But a moon-faced man with a thin black moustache came out of the kitchen to greet them and escort them to a beautifully appointed table.

"Sorry to be late, Louis," Nicolas Panos apologized.

"Do not worry, Monsieur. Your secretary telephoned and explained. I was sorry to hear of your sister's misfortune." The patron held a chair for Alex to sit down. "The hors d'oeuvres will be ready in a moment, but if you wish for an aperitif, please make it a light one."

"You don't want us to spoil our palates, eh? Very well, Louis, we will have nothing. You may bring the wine instead."

The patron smiled and hurried away, and Alex looked tentatively at the man opposite her.

"I didn't know you were late tonight because of family reasons. You should have told me."

"You gave me no chance."

She knew she was being put in her place but felt she deserved it. "Was it bad news?"

"My sister had a baby last week, and I learned tonight that the child has died."

"I'm so sorry. If I had known you were upset, I wouldn't have been rude to you."

"It is a pity you need the excuse of bereavement to

apologize for your bad manners." The words were quietly spoken but they brought the color to her cheeks.

"I said I was sorry, Mr. Panos. A gentleman would have accepted the apology without belaboring the point."

"What makes you think I'm a gentleman?"

"Nothing you have done so far," she said crossly.

He stared at her, then threw back his head and laughed. It was a loud, wholehearted sound of un-monitored amusement, a laugh that brought to mind Greek peasants dancing and stamping their feet in a taverna.

"I find it difficult to be annoyed with you for long, Alex." He spoke her name without any self-consciousness, as if he had been thinking of her in this way for a long time. "You are so refreshingly honest even when you're insulting me!"

She was glad the arrival of their first course prevented her from replying, for much attention was given to the presentation of the dish; a mound of baby langoustes nestling on a bed of what looked like thick yellow cream but turned out to be a tarragon-flavored mayonnaise, whipped to aerated lightness.

It was a simple course, yet her first mouthful told Alex she had never before tasted langoustes like these.

"Louis gets them direct from the Adriatic," her escort vouchsafed. "They are still the best in the world."

"Are you interested in food?"

"Very much so. And in wine, too. Eating and drinking are two of life's pleasures." One of his eyebrows lifted. "There are other pleasures, too."

"Sex and business," she stated, looking him fully in

the face. "Though I'm sure that with you, business comes first."

He smiled, and his eyebrow rose even higher. It was a gesture she already recognized as one of his mannerisms, and an extremely attractive one, too, for it gave him a faintly sardonic air.

"You are a girl who does not mince her words," he said. "I am glad of that."

"I am in the acting profession, Mr. Panos, and used to frankness."

"All women are actresses!" he replied. "And most of them would have looked coy when I made that remark."

"You must know a strange breed of women, then."

"You are beginning to make me realize that!"

He made no further overt remarks during the meal, and instead regaled her with anecdotes about his work and the people he met. He was a fluent conversationalist with bite to his wit, and he made everything he described come vividly to life.

It was only when coffee and brandy were set before them that he turned to the subject of his cousin.

"I know he has said he wishes to marry you. No doubt he has also told you he will let nothing stand in his way."

"Are you asking me or telling me?" she questioned.

"Telling you." The reply was calm. "Leon has fallen in love so many times in the past that I know his lines by heart."

"You are also inferring he will fall in love many more times in the future?"

"I do not know that. His love for you may well be the first genuine emotion he has experienced. You are beautiful enough to arouse such a feeling in a man."

"I didn't use my looks to trap him, Mr. Panos. Leon did all the running."

"That is an excellent way to hold his attention. He is a man who likes the chase."

"I didn't deliberately play hard to get, either," she snapped. "It wasn't my intention to trap him!"

"If you were foolish enough to marry him, *you* would be the one who was trapped!"

Alex tried but failed to make sense of this. "Why?"

"Because Leon isn't the man for you—nor for any girl of intelligence."

"And I'm obviously intelligent," she said sarcastically. "Though it didn't require all that much to foresee *your* behavior. You've wasted your time with me, Mr. Panos. I don't need any financial inducement to dissuade me from marrying your cousin. I have already turned him down!"

"There is no need to have false pride with me," he said quietly. "I don't blame you for falling in love with him. Many women have."

"I'm not in love with him," she insisted, "and I have no intention of marrying him."

"You haven't given that impression to Leon." The words were soft but exasperated.

"Because he doesn't believe any girl could ever turn him down. Lack of confidence isn't one of his failings!"

The man said nothing, but there was a brooding quality in his face that suggested he was trying to assess her words. Watching him, it suddenly became important for her to make him believe she had not given her heart to such an inconsequential young man as Leon.

"Please believe I'm telling you the truth, Mr. Panos. I

like Leon, but I don't love him and I repeatedly told him so. Unfortunately he didn't think I meant it."

"He might have done so if you had stopped seeing him."

It was a valid comment and had to be answered. "That was what I finally realized the last time I saw him. I was making plans to return to England when I discovered you had sent him to Greece."

"Leon never told me you were leaving France."

"I had no chance to tell him. You sent him away without any warning."

"You can't blame us."

His use of the word "us" brought home to her that he was here as a representative of his family, and her scorn for their high-handed way of running people's lives made her lose her temper.

"I suppose I should feel flattered you consider me such a threat to Greek solidarity. But in a world of diminishing horizons, I find such insularity repugnant."

"There is more than insularity at stake," he rapped. "There is one's cultural pattern and heritage. Or perhaps you don't set any value on that?"

"Continual inbreeding leads to senility! Even the strongest culture and the longest line can be strengthened by new blood!"

Nicolas Panos stared down at the table, giving the impression that he was deep in thought. "If you are generalizing, then I agree with you. But we are talking about Leon—and he happens to need a girl from his own background. One must be capable of great understanding in order to overcome the obstacles of a different race and religion. Love alone is not enough. And Leon does not have the—"

"I have already told you I'm not going to marry him! When he comes back from Greece, I will tell him so again."

"It may not be necessary for you to do so."

"You mean I'll be in England before he gets back?"

He shook his head and gave an unexpectedly warm smile. It took years from his age and made her aware what a heavy burden it was to be the son of Christoff Panos.

"That wasn't what I meant at all, Alex. The opposite, in fact."

The look in his eyes made his meaning obvious. He wanted her. Not as a wife, of course. It went without saying that a girl unsuitable for Leon would be even more unsuitable for the Panos heir—but as another scalp to add to his long line of conquests. Swallowing her bitterness, she pushed back her chair.

"It's late, Mr. Panos. I would like to go home."

Silently he stood up, signaled the patron that he was leaving, and led her to the car.

The journey back to Cabray was equally silent. The man concentrated on the road, driving fast this time but showing such superb control of the car that Alex was not afraid.

She was glad he had made no further pretence of interest in her once she had assured him she had no designs on Leon, though it was not flattering to her ego. Still, he was used to beautiful women and one more, or one less, obviously made no difference to him.

A lamp glimmered in the living room of the cottage as they finally came to a stop by the rickety gate, and, still without a word, he escorted her across the uneven grass to the bottom of the terrace.

He put his hand under her elbow to guide her up the steps. It was his first physical contact with her, and she was conscious of the light touch of his fingers on her skin and their surprising warmth. At the door, he stopped.

"I'm not going to lead with my chin and ask if you enjoyed the evening," he said drily. "But I hope you at least enjoyed the meal!"

Without waiting for her reply, he went back down the steps. At once he was absorbed by the darkness, but as she unlocked the door and glanced over her shoulder, she saw the dip of his headlamps as he drove along the narrow lane.

So much for her belief—unrealized until this moment—that he would ask to see her again! He had fulfilled his duty to his aunt and could now proceed with his own life. The thought should have pleased her, but with the perversity of the truly feminine heart, she was inexplicably disappointed.

Chapter Six

Saturday brought such an influx of customers that Eleanor decided to open on Sunday, too. Alex hid her dismay at losing her only day of rest, ashamed of herself for feeling tired when her godmother —who could give her thirty years at least—showed no signs of fatigue. Perhaps Eleanor's urge to increase her bank account also served to increase her energy.

"By all means, let's open tomorrow," Alex said with forced pleasure. "But we'll have to do some baking. There isn't a cake or biscuit left."

For the next few hours, the smell of yeast and spices filled the air around the cottage, and it was midnight before the oven was finally turned off. Lying under the eaves in her small bedroom, Alex was too tired to sleep and, without any prompting, Nicolas Panos came into her mind. How incredibly good-looking he was, and how feeble Leon seemed in comparison.

Determinedly she focused her mind on the morrow. It looked like being another lovely day—as most of the days were, now that summer was upon them. It would be nice to live here permanently. Not in Cabray, but on the coast, with a view of the sea. No doubt the Panos villa overlooked the sea and had a wonderful view, too, though the heir to it was probably too busy with his business commitments to notice the prospect.

Angry with herself for thinking of him again, she firmly started to count sheep, giving that up, too, when she found they all had glossy black hair and heavy-lidded, impenetrable eyes.

Sleep took a long time to come, and, because of it, she was downstairs later than usual the next morning to find that her godmother had already dusted the tables and chairs on the terrace.

"It'll be annoying if no one turns up today," Alex murmured, stretching her arms above her head and enjoying the warm air. "We might find we did all that baking for nothing!"

"Oh yes?" Eleanor grinned and pointed to where several people were descending the lane towards the cottage.

These were only the first of an influx, and, by noon, they had served as many customers as they normally did during an entire day.

Alex rushed from one table to another, all the time aware of the table at the far end of the terrace which Nicolas Panos had made his own. A young couple were sitting there today, and she turned away from them. It was stupid of her to think Leon's cousin would come here again. Now that he no longer regarded her as a threat to family unity, he had obliterated her from his mind.

As she thought this, she saw him walking towards her across the grass. Her breath caught in her throat, and she knew an intense longing to run away and hide. Forcing down her ridiculous fear, she waited for him to reach her. As he did, she was forced to tilt back her head to look at him. He really was exceptionally tall for a Greek and appeared even taller because of the proud way he carried himself.

"I wasn't expecting all this," he said in hard tones, waving a hand in the direction of the crowded tables. "I thought you closed on a Sunday?"

"Normally we do, but it seemed silly to miss a day."

"It is even siller not to have a rest."

"It's kind of you to be concerned about my welfare, Mr. Panos, but it isn't necessary."

His lips set tight, and he flung an irritable glance about him.

"I'm afraid there are no tables free at the moment," she said quickly.

"I didn't come here as a customer. I came only to see *you*."

Her hands clenched at her sides. "Didn't I convince you the other night?"

"Convince me of what?"

"That I don't want to marry Leon."

"If you say it often enough I might believe you."

"Why should I lie to you?"

"Pride?" he challenged.

"I fail to see what pride has to do with it." She

waited for him to explain, but his shrug indicated an end of the subject.

"Don't tell me this rush goes on until five?" he muttered. "It will drive me crazy!"

"You don't need to stay here."

"I have come to see you, and I've every intention of waiting. Get rid of everyone!"

She stared at him in astonishment and angrily he glared at her. Then his mouth started to twitch, and all at once he was smiling.

"Forgive me, Alex. It was a foolish thing to say. But I had assumed you would be free today, and I am annoyed that you are not."

"Actually we won't be serving any more customers. We only planned to open for the morning."

His glance raked the tables. "Then you should be free within an hour. I will take a walk round the garden and return later."

"Mind how you go," she said involuntarily as he moved towards the steps. "The stones are crumbling and some of the terrace isn't safe."

"You should get it repaired."

"It's a major job," she replied, "which is one of the reasons we opened today."

He flashed her a sharp look, and she colored, hoping he did not see her remark as a hint for money. How awful if he did! Yet if this were so, it would account for his disbelieving her when she had said she did not want to marry Leon. It would also account for his being here today. The knowledge depressed her and, unwilling to dwell on it, she busied herself preparing bills and clearing away tables as soon as their occupants stood up to leave.

It was one-thirty before the terrace was finally deserted, and she leaned against the balustrade and pushed the damp hair away from her forehead. She was more exhausted than she had believed possible and could think of nothing better than to relax on a sandy beach. The sweep of the hills around her, broken by the silver-green of olive trees and the darker shapes of conifers, gave her a hemmed-in feeling, and she longed for a sight of the sea. There was something restful about water and waves lapping on a shore.

"What are you thinking about?" A deep voice, with a slight but definite accent, brought her spinning round to see Nicolas directly behind her.

"Just longing for a sight of the sea." Her own voice was breathless and she was aware of a sudden difficulty with her breathing. What was there about this man that made her so conscious of every bone in her body?

"I will take you to the sea, Alex. Collect your swimming costume."

"There's no need for you to ask me out."

"There is every need."

"But—"

"*My* need," he said softly. "Stop arguing, and do as I say."

Trembling, she turned away from him. He was right; it was pointless to argue. Besides, there was nothing momentous in being asked out a second time by the same man.

"Give me half an hour," she murmured.

"Take your time. I will wait no matter how long you are."

Her trembling increased and she hurried away, unwilling to analyze her reaction.

She kept her mind a blank as she showered and changed into a simple white cotton dress. She applied fresh lipstick and mascara, ran a comb through her long, corn-gold hair, and was downstairs again within twenty minutes.

The terrace was deserted, but voices came from the kitchen and she found Nicolas Panos and her god-mother sitting either side of the pine table. A plate of cold meat and salad was set out, and he looked at Alex and pointed to it.

"I thought you would be in need of some sustenance."

"I'm not hungry, thank you," she lied, but she received such a hard look from him that she sat down and took up her fork. "What about you?"

"I had a late breakfast and I rarely eat during the day. When I am working, I generally carry straight through until dinner. Are you enjoying it?" he asked abruptly, and she paused, fork in the air, before she nodded, disconcerted by his solicitude.

He did not make any further conversation with her while she ate but talked to Eleanor instead, managing to learn a great deal about the woman by asking a few astute questions.

"Are you always so curious about people?" Alex asked him as, with the cottage behind, they drove towards the coast.

"Only if they interest me."

"Why are you interested in my godmother?"

"I am interested in everyone and everything that concerns you."

"Why?"

"Because it will help me to know you better."

"Is that why you came here today?"

"Do you find that so difficult to understand? You obviously do not look in your mirror."

"You mean you find me attractive," she said with deliberate flatness.

"I find you beautiful," he corrected.

"I'm sure there's a surfeit of beautiful women in your life. Why bother with *me*?"

"You have more to offer than beauty. I also like to talk to you."

"You mean you like me for my mind," she said drily.

"Without it, you would be no different from the other women I have known—whom you take delight in remembering!"

She reddened and said nothing.

"I hope you have brought your swimming costume?" he asked after a moment.

She nodded but did not ask where they would be swimming, and, as if piqued by her lack of interest, he said: "Don't you want to know where I'm taking you?"

"Would it make any difference if I said I didn't want to go?"

"No! When I make up my mind about something, I rarely change it."

"That's why I didn't ask you!"

He chuckled. "You seem to know me very well, little one."

It was an unusual endearment, and it established a friendliness between them that she had not felt to be there. She relaxed against the seat and closed her eyes. The movement of the car was hypnotic, the sound of the tires on the tarmac a pleasant swish, which, together with the warmth of the day, sent her into a dreamless slumber.

It was the abrupt cessation of sound that awakened her, and she opened her eyes to find herself looking into black, fathomless ones. Instinctively she pressed back against the seat and he straightened away from her.

"You feel refreshed?" he enquired.

"Yes, thank you. But I'm sorry for falling asleep. It was rude of me."

"I like having you asleep beside me."

Blushing, she sat up and looked around. They were parked in a semicircular drive, to the left of which lay an enormous white, two-storied villa. She had no time to study it, for her host came 'round to her side of the car and opened the door for her.

Skirting the front wall, he led the way 'round the house to a scene of breathtaking splendor. A tiled terrace, arched and columned like a Moorish palace, stretched for some two hundred feet along the southern flank of the villa. It was bordered by a lush expanse of lawn that seemed to go on forever before stopping by a railing which, she knew, gave onto the edge of the cliff. Below it lay the sea, sparkling blue and dotted with the white of boats.

"Come and take a better look," he said and moved lightly forward.

Alex followed him to the railing and, peering over, saw that steps had been hewn into the rock. They led down to a jetty that had been carved out of the cliff's edge. A couple of motorboats were moored there and, without being told, she knew he had brought her to his home.

"Do you like it?" he asked.

"Who wouldn't? It's beautiful."

"Good. I will show you the house itself. I am very proud of it."

"Did you design it?"

"I had the sense to choose an architect who agreed to incorporate my own ideas."

"That doesn't surprise me!"

"Puss, puss," he cautioned. "If you keep sharpening your claws on me, I will have to cut them!"

He caught her hand and held it up, but she snatched it away and ran back to the terrace. Peering into the rooms that lay behind it, she saw they were filled with sunshine, and, tilting her head up, she noticed that the arched roof of the terrace allowed this to happen.

"Most of the people who live here," she exclaimed as her host joined her, "like to keep the sun out of their houses."

"Only because they object to the heat."

"Don't you?"

"When I need to be cool, I switch on the air conditioning."

"Do you live here the whole year?" she asked and was immediately annoyed at showing her curiosity, for he gave a slow smile.

"That is the first personal question you have asked me. Does it mean your dislike of me is beginning to lessen?"

"I never said I disliked you, Mr. Panos."

"I would believe that more easily if you called me Nico."

"I don't know you well enough to call you by your name."

"We live in an age when first names are almost *de rigeur*," he protested. "And in your profession particularly so."

"That's true," she conceded and went with him into the house.

She found herself in a living room of gigantic proportions. Half a dozen settees and an equal number of armchairs in varying shades of brown suede—from palest cream to richest sienna—were ranged across a white and gold marble floor, redeemed from coldness by a scattering of beautiful rugs: small carpets in reality, though the vastness of the room diminished their size. Silken drapery in hues of peacock blue and green billowed along the glass wall through which she had come in, while the wall opposite was of paneled wood and was covered with paintings. Even at a quick glance she recognized Matisse, Manet, and Cézanne.

"Beautiful, aren't they?" Nicolas waved a hand at them, irritating her by his frank enthusiasm for his own possessions.

"If you like the French Impressionists," she said coolly. "Personally, my taste is more eclectic."

"So is mine, Miss Sharp Tongue! But where better to show off the Impressionists than down here? Don't forget it was the light of Provence that inspired so many of them to throw away their dark palettes and use brilliant colors." He stopped and looked faintly apologetic. "But I mustn't lecture you. Painting is a hobby of mine, and I tend to resent criticism of my taste!"

"I didn't mean to sound rude," she said carefully, and moved across to have a closer look at a Cézanne. "I've never even seen a reproduction of this one!"

"It has never been photographed. It was in a private

collection in Lugano when I got hold of it." He came to stand beside her, his face turned up to the picture. "I first learned of its existence four years ago, but it wasn't until last month that I managed to persuade its owner to sell it to me."

"I can't understand anyone wanting a painting so much."

"Do you not like possessions?"

"I'm more interested in people."

"I can be possessive about people, too." He turned his head to look at her. "If I want someone, I will do anything to get them."

"You make yourself sound very ruthless."

"Do I?" He was surprised. "I prefer to think that I'm single-minded. Ruthlessness implies cruelty."

"Maybe you *are* cruel!"

He smiled, his teeth very white in his tanned face. "I will leave you to tell me if I am."

Unwilling to answer, she wandered the room to look at the other paintings, but he opened a door into the hall and motioned her to follow him. The floor here was also marble, but in black and white, which continued up the shallow staircase that wound up to the first floor.

"I don't need to see the rest of the house," she said quickly.

"Are you afraid of going into the bedrooms with me?" His expression was baiting, but she refused to rise to it and went back to the living room.

"I thought you promised me a swim, Mr. Panos?"

"Nico," he reminded her. "And since you're afraid to go upstairs and change, you will have to make do with a cabaña!"

Feeling foolish, which was exactly what he had intended, she went with him across the lawn. Expecting to be led down the rocky steps to the sea, she was surprised to be taken through a belt of trees and along a winding path to where a section of the rock had been carved away to form a vast ledge. Here a magnificent free-form swimming pool gleamed like an aquamarine. To one side of it stood a small Grecian building which she correctly guessed to be the changing rooms, while all around were *chaises-longues* and hammocks in scarlet and blue.

Left alone to don her swimsuit, she spent a little time examining her surroundings. There were four separate cabins and showers and a refrigerator stocked with cold drinks, fresh fruit, and champagne. There was also a telephone, a sign that the Panos men never allowed themselves to relax totally.

There were footsteps outside, and she retreated into one of the cabins, afraid that Nicolas was coming to see why she was so long. Irrationally, she was embarrassed at appearing before him in a bikini, and it required all her *sangfroid* to stroll out to the pool.

He was nowhere to be seen, and she momentarily relaxed, stiffening again as his head bobbed up almost at her feet, and she looked down and saw him in the water. His body was the same golden bronze as his face, and, as he heaved himself up on to the side, she saw the ripple of perfectly coordinated muscles. He wore brief white shorts and exhibited none of the self-consciousness from which she was suffering.

"Do you swim?" he asked nonchalantly.

"Like a fish with one fin!"

She heard his chuckle as she dived into the water. Only as she started to swim did she realize it was sea water, and she could not help reflecting on the benefits of wealth. A house on Cap Ferrat with its own private beach, in addition to an Olympic-size swimming pool with sea water pumped up from three hundred feet below.

"A penny for your thoughts?" Unseen, Nicolas had slipped into the water and swam beneath its surface to reemerge beside her.

"I was thinking how marvelous it must be to be rich enough to afford all this."

"Wealth has its compensations!"

"You make it sound as if it has disadvantages, too!"

"It has. One cannot possess a fortune without being committed to take care of it."

"You're bearing up well under the strain!"

"I was prepared for it from birth," he said dryly.

"I'll never be able to think of money as a great heritage," she mused. "It's never been that important to me."

"Yet you like luxurious things?"

"Certainly. But I don't mind not having them."

He opened his mouth as if to speak, paused, and then palpably changed the subject. "Come, Alex. I will race you the length of the pool."

"That's no race," she protested. "It's a foregone conclusion!"

"I won't use my arms—just my legs!"

With a laugh, she accepted the challenge, but even so they touched the blue-tiled wall together and then hauled themselves up to sit on the side. She shook the water from her hair and tried to stifle her breathlessness.

"You swim well," he commented and gave her the favor of a long, intent stare that traveled the length of her body and made her aware of every curve she possessed. "Your figure is as beautiful without clothes as with them," he said finally.

"I'm not nude," she retorted.

"As good as makes no difference. Those two wisps of pink cotton don't leave much to the imagination."

"And yours is obviously working overtime!"

"Are you surprised?"

"Why should I be? You're a Greek!"

With a throaty laugh, he pushed her back into the water. Not expecting the assault, she swallowed a mouthful, and he dived in and hauled her, coughing and spluttering, back on to the side.

"Next time you start ladling out the insults," he warned, "make sure you aren't in such a precarious position!"

For the rest of the afternoon, they swam and sunbathed. Tea was brought to them by a butler, with milk for herself and lemon for Nicolas. She sat on a sunbed, sipping the tea and staring out at the horizon. A faint breeze lifted the blonde tendrils of hair from her forehead and blew against the long, damp tresses that lay on her shoulders.

It was an idyllic way to pass an afternoon, and she wished she could spend more of them like this. But to do so would be dangerous; Nicolas was too attractive a man for any woman to be long in his company and still retain her heart.

She glanced at him. He lay with his face turned up to the sun and his eyes closed. It gave her an opportunity to study him without being observed, and she enjoyed the handsome picture he made. His lids lifted, and dark eyes stared into hers. Quickly she turned away, aware of him sitting up and stretching.

"That little sleep did me good," he murmured. "I had business calls from the States until four o'clock this morning."

"So late!"

He smiled. "My father can manage with four hours' sleep a night. He cannot understand why anyone should need more."

"Does he still take an active interest in the business?"

"Not as much as he did. That means he only works twelve hours a day!"

"Are you the same?"

"No. Life is too short to spend it all working. There are more important things." He looked around him. "Spending time with my friends, for instance, and enjoying this place."

"Yet you're still single?"

"I have never loved a woman sufficiently to want to spend the rest of my life with her."

Carefully Alex picked at a thread on the linen cover of her sunbed. "I'm surprised you see marriage in permanent terms. Most people in your position don't."

"How you love to generalize! You should try to see people as individuals and not stereotypes."

"Rich people tend to follow a particular pattern."

"All people follow a pattern." He eyed her. "I suppose you see me as being incapable of love?"

"I think you're very cynical about it," she corrected. "Look at the way you prejudged my attitude to Leon."

"Only because I prejudged Leon! Until now, all his girlfriends have been—but no, we will not talk of him.

We will talk of me—which I prefer." His smile was sharp. "I agree I am cynical. But that doesn't mean I have lost all my illusions. You, for example, are helping to keep them alive. You had a chance to marry a member of the Panos family, yet you turned it down because you didn't want wealth without love. If that hasn't restored my faith in feminine nature, nothing will!"

She knew he was teasing her but also sensed a sneer behind his words. "I know you find it hard to believe anyone can turn down such an opportunity, but I assure you I don't regret it. There are other things I consider far more important."

"Such as?"

"Doing work you enjoy. Having genuine friends and not needing to worry if they like you for what you are and not for what you can give them! There's even pleasure in having to save up for things you want. I don't expect you to understand that," she added. "You've always been able to buy everything you desired."

"Not everything. Some things I have to wait for . . . to plan for."

She was reluctant to think he was referring to herself and deliberately said: "Like waiting four years to get that Cézanne?"

He nodded, though the gleam in his eyes belied the movement. Involuntarily she shivered, and he misread it as a sign that she was cold and suggested they change and return to the terrace.

"What would you like to do this evening?" he asked when they were seated there, watching the sun slowly sink into the horizon.

"I thought you were taking me back to the cottage."

"Not for hours yet. I warned your godmother not to expect you back early."

"I'm not dressed for going anywhere except the beach."

"I refuse to tell you that in your cotton dress you look lovelier than any woman in a ball gown. If you don't know it already, you're a fool!" He leaned towards her. "I assume Leon has already taken you to l'Oasis at La Napoule?"

She nodded. "Does that mean *you* won't take me there?"

"I like to be different," he said calmly.

"You'll have your work cut out," she said, amused by what she saw as his first display of childishness. "The one thing Leon knows is every good restaurant along the coast!"

"Not every one," he disagreed. "You had never been to Louis's before."

"That's true. And it was marvelous. How is it that Leon doesn't know it?"

"It's too quiet for him. When he takes out a beautiful girl, he likes to show her off."

"Do you prefer to hide me?"

His eyes narrowed. "When I am getting to know someone, I do not like to be with them in a crowd. I prefer to concentrate on them alone. As I intend to concentrate on you."

Nervously, she edged back in her seat, and he saw the movement and frowned.

"I have been many years finding you, Alex, and, now that I have, I intend to make up for lost time."

She waited for him to continue, but he settled back

in his chair and stared out at the view. It was foolhardy
to read too much into what he had said, and she reminded herself that he was only intrigued by her because she had held out against his charm. For this
reason alone he might want to have an affair with her.
Yet hadn't she made it clear she was not interested in
that sort of relationship? Or did he still think she was
putting on an act with him?

"I won't go to bed with you, Nicolas." The words
had no sooner come into her mind than she said them,
and he sat up straight and stared at her.

"I do not remember asking you," he said coldly.

"You know what I mean."

"I do. But what *you* have just said shows you have
no idea what *I* mean. Once again you are generalizing
about me instead of using your intelligence."

"Perhaps I believe what the gossip columnists have
said about you."

"What is past is past," he said tersely. "A man
changes as he grows older."

She could not prevent herself from smiling, and,
seeing it, he became angry.

"You think I'm lying, don't you, Alex? That is why
you're amused."

"Not at all. I was smiling at your vehemence. You
have a way of making your opinions sound like irrefutable facts!"

"My opinions *are* irrefutable facts!"

This time she laughed outright, though the sound
died in her throat as he reached out and drew her hand
to his lips.

"I love it when you make fun of me," he said hus-

kily. "No woman has ever done that. You *will* let me
see you each day, won't you?"

Surprised, she had no time to prevaricate. "I suppose so—for as long as I'm here."

"Where are you going?"

"Back to England. If I stay away too long, my name
will be forgotten."

"Is it well known?" He frowned. "I can't say I've
heard of it."

"You wouldn't have. I'm an unknown."

"But you are ambitious?"

"Of course." Even as she spoke, she knew she was
lying. For some inexplicable reason, she was no longer
excited by the prospect of a successful career on the
stage. She caught at her lower lip, puzzled by her reaction.

Nicolas did not appear to find much pleasure in her
answer either, for he looked stern and distant. "Are
you a woman who puts her career before a home and
family?"

"I think it's possible to have both."

"No man would be willing to play second fiddle to
a theater or film studio!"

"I'll make sure I marry a man who *is*."

"Can you be so certain of guiding your heart?"

The flippant answer she was on the point of making
died as she saw the seriousness of his gaze, and again
she wished she could tell what he was thinking.

"Of course I can't be sure," she said. "If I could
have guided my heart, I'd have directed it towards
Leon. As you once said, he isn't a man many women
would turn down."

Nicolas jumped up angrily. "I'm being serious, Alex, and all you do is joke."

"I don't know why you're so cross," she said helplessly.

"Don't you? Don't you know I haven't been able to get you out of my mind since I met you? That you come between me and my work? Christ!" he swore. "I am obsessed with you!"

Incredulously she stared at him, knowing he was speaking the truth and understanding why he was bewildered by it. He had sought her out in order to prevent her from marrying his cousin and instead had succumbed to her himself. But his way of appeasing his desire would be far different from Leon's.

"Why do you look surprised" he demanded. "Don't you know what a desirable woman you are?"

"I hadn't realized you were so susceptible."

"Generally I'm not. But with you . . . . " He leaned down and placed his hands on either side of her chair. "Within a few moments of meeting you, I knew you were different from what I had expected."

Again she tried and failed to read his enigmatic expression. "What did Leon say about me?"

"It is unimportant," he shrugged. "All that matters is what *I* say." He leaned closer still, and she felt his breath on her cheek. "Aren't you going to say something nice to me in return? You are not usually a dumb blonde!"

"At the moment I am! Your compliments have stunned me."

"I don't like you thinking of my words as compliments. I am serious."

She longed to ask what serious meant but could not

bring herself to do so. Anyway, in a few weeks she would be returning to London, and she doubted if his desire for her was strong enough to propel him to come after her. Once she was out of his life, some other beautiful woman would come into it. All this virile and handsome man wanted was a temporary playmate. And that was a role she definitely did not intend to play. Angered by her thoughts, she shook her head and a tress of hair swung out and brushed his cheek.

The touch of it was his undoing, and with a low murmur he pulled her to her feet and into his arms.

The moment his lips touched hers she knew he was a man of experience. It was apparent in his hold, in the strength of his arms, and the gentleness of his hands as they moved across her back and down her spine to encircle her waist and draw her closer still. And all the while his mouth moved softly upon hers, arousing her to a response she had never before given to any man. His kiss deepened and, recognizing the danger of it, she turned her head away from his.

"Don't," she whispered. "Please don't." For an instant, she thought he was not going to take any notice, then his hands dropped away from her and he stepped back.

"I won't say I'm sorry," he said softly. "You wanted me to kiss you."

"I most certainly didn't!"

His eyes glittered like burning coals. "You are lying, Alex. You *do* want me."

She forced a laugh from lips that still burned from his touch. "Then at least you no longer believe I want Leon. That's *some* progress!"

The burning look in his eyes intensified. "Even if you were crazy about him, I would make you forget him."

"You don't suffer from an inferiority complex, do you?"

"I know that women find me attractive," he said calmly. "But since, for some reason best known to you, you are reluctant to admit it, I suggest we drop the subject until such time as you can be honest with me." He moved along the terrace. "Come, we will go out to dinner. If I remain here alone with you, I won't be responsible for my actions."

For the rest of the evening he treated her as if she were an amusing and well-liked sister. Occasionally there was a glimpse of something else in his eyes, but it went as quickly as it came, and she sensed he was exercising all his self-control. She sensed, too, that it was a control he had rarely had to exercise before. Women undoubtedly fell for him like ninepins and would have done so without the added inducement of the Panos fortune. How easily she herself could succumb to his charm, and only the knowledge that it would bring her lasting unhappiness helped her to keep her emotions in check. It was a good thing she would shortly be leaving France.

But none of her thoughts were put into words, and she responded to his banter in a fashion as lighthearted as his own, managing to maintain the mood as he drove her back to Cabray shortly before midnight. This time as he said goodnight, he told her he would call for her the following evening, taking it for granted she was willing to be with him.

"I may not be able to call for you myself," he added

as he left her at the door of the cottage. "I have some people flying in from Paris and I will be with them until late. If I can't get away from them in time, I'll send my chauffeur for you."

"Why don't we leave the evening open? If you're busy, you might prefer to—"

"I don't intend to waste a day by not seeing you," he interrupted. "Now I've found you, I won't let you go."

As she lay in bed, she hugged his words alone, wishing they augured something different from what she knew they did. "I won't let you go." How wonderfully final that sounded. Yet all it meant was a few weeks' or a few months' infatuation with her before he became obsessed by someone else. If she had any sense, she would refuse to see him again.

Yet sense had deserted her, now that her senses had taken over. All she wanted was to feel the thrill of knowing Nicolas desired her. For the short time she remained here, she would see him and enjoy his company. Once she was back in England and among her own friends, her natural intelligence would return, and he would become a pleasant memory that would inexorably fade.

Chapter Seven

For the next fortnight, *Alex saw* Nicolas every day, and Eleanor made no secret of her fear that her goddaughter was playing with fire and would get hurt.

"I thought you were going back to London soon," she said one afternoon.

"I have to wait until Sherry's friend finds another flat."

"That's only an excuse. You told me she only needed a week's notice before going."

"She'd pack up at once if I asked her to," Alex admitted, "but I don't want to leave here yet."

"Because of Nicolas?"

"Yes."

"There's no future in it."

"I know. But at least I'll have lovely memories!"

"Or lovely heartache," Eleanor grunted. "If I were in your shoes, I'd pack up and run!"

"It's too late," Alex said slowly. "I love him."

There was an appreciable pause. "Are you sure it's the man himself, and not what he represents?"

"His position, you mean? Surely you know me better than that."

"I wasn't thinking of his wealth." Eleanor brushed this aspect aside. "But a man in his position has an enormous amount of power, and it gives him a charisma, makes going out with him a *coup* that any girl would find desirable."

"Maybe his power does give him a charisma," Alex agreed, "but there's much more to him than that. Even without being important, he'd still have the same things I love. His wit and intelligence, his attitude towards life. He feels about things the way I do and he isn't afraid to show his emotion. If he wants. . . . " She stopped. "It's hard to put it into words."

"You aren't doing too badly," Eleanor said drily. "But I still think you'd be wiser to run."

"I'll still love him."

"You'll forget him more easily if you leave now. Think about it."

Alex did so later that evening as she sat opposite Nicolas in a restaurant overlooking Cannes harbor. She knew that even if she left him at this very moment, she would remember him all her life.

"You look very lovely and relaxed," Nicolas commented, raising his glass in her direction.

"You make me feel both," she smiled. "You have what the newspapers call 'a way with women'."

"I wish I could make you forget my reputation,"

he growled. "What do I have to do to convince you I'm in love with you?"

"Marry me," were the words that hovered on her lips, but she could not bring herself to say them. Instead she turned her eyes to the harbor, where boats large and small bobbed gently on the water.

"Do you have a yacht?" she asked for want of something to say.

"I have several hundred ships and a large number of supertankers. But no yacht of my own. I prefer houses."

"I'm sure you have those in the plural."

"Four, as a matter of fact. But I'm willing to buy a yacht if you'd like one!"

She stared at him and then laughed. "Do you always pander to your girlfriends' tastes?"

"Of course." He reached across the table for her hand. "This is the first time you've called yourself my girlfriend. I hope you mean it?"

"Only in the literal sense of the word," she replied with commendable presence of mind.

"One day I'll—"

His sentence was cut short by his name being called by a young girl in her mid-twenties who came over to them. Small and slightly plump, she had an astonishingly beautiful face of classic proportions. That she was Greek was apparent in her accent and coloring, and also that she knew Nicolas extremely well, for she was holding onto his arm with affection.

"We've all been wondering what's happened to you these last few weeks, Nico. No one has seen you around, and you haven't been taking any calls."

"You malign me, Elena. I reply to all my telephone calls."

"You mean your secretary does," the girl pouted. "I invited you to dinner twice, and he refused both times."

"I have been busy."

"I'm sure you have." The girl's smile included Alex, but there was no jealousy in the look, merely curiosity. "How is Leon?" she asked Nicolas. "Have you managed to solve his little problem?"

"Yes."

It was a clipped sound but not sharp enough to warn Elena she was treading on dangerous ground.

She looked at Alex and grinned. "Do you know Leon?"

"Yes."

"Isn't it typical of him to get involved with some girl down here and then have Nico come to his rescue?"

"I don't think Leon needs rescuing," Alex said quietly.

"His fiancée wouldn't agree with you—if she knew!" Elena looked at Nicolas again. "How long is Leon staying with her?"

"I'm not sure."

The words were even more clipped, and Elena became aware of it, though she misconstrued the reason. "Don't tell me Leon's still involved with the other girl?"

"I've already told you it's finished."

"How much did it cost you? Or did you pretend *you'd* fallen for her?"

"Excuse me," Alex whispered, and, pushing back her chair, she moved blindly away from the table.

"Alex!"

Ignoring Nicolas's call, she increased her pace. As she reached the sidewalk, she saw him fling some money on the table and, knowing he would soon be coming after her, she began to run.

There were no taxis in sight, and she lunged down a side turning, not caring where she went as long as she was out of sight.

So, after all, Nicolas had been pretending he had fallen in love with her! What an idiot she was not to have seen through his behavior! She should have realized he was too used to easy conquests to waste time with someone who was playing hard to get unless he had an ulterior motive for doing so. Well, now she knew what that motive was: afraid that she was still hoping to marry Leon, he had decided that the best way to make sure she didn't was to have her fall in love with himself instead.

Yet surely he could have achieved the same result by telling her Leon already had a fiancée? Or had he been afraid that if she found this out, she would cause a scandal? Tears poured down her cheeks, and she stopped running and searched in her bag for a handkerchief. As she put it away a taxi cruised by, and she flagged it down.

On the long drive back to Cabray, she continued to flagellate herself with memories of Nicolas. But as the hilltop village came into sight, she vowed that after she had told Eleanor what had transpired this evening, she would never mention his name.

The driver slowed down to ask exactly where she wished to go, and, knowing he would grumble at having to massacre his tires on the unmade road that led to the cottage, she asked him to stop at the top of the lane. As he drove off, she carefully picked her way along the path.

It was only when she was halfway down that she noticed the car parked by the entrance to the garden and discerned the tall figure of a man standing by the bonnet. Nicolas must have driven here straight from the restaurant. Her heart began pounding, but she walked resolutely forward, increasing her pace as she reached the car and went to walk past it.

"No you don't!" Nicolas grated, barring her way. "The least you can do is to hear my side of the story."

"I've heard enough of your stories!"

"You're still going to hear this one."

"I won't!" Sidestepping him, she ran across the grass.

"Alex, wait!"

Nicolas raced after her, and, afraid he would catch her before she reached the cottage, she changed direction and ran down the garden towards the stream that lay at the far end of the property, hoping to lose him in the tangle of trees that bordered it. Then she would be able to work her way back toward the house without his seeing her. But he was fleeter of foot than she had expected, and she heard him gaining on her. Wildly she veered towards the terrace, praying Eleanor had left the back door unlocked.

"Alex!" he called again. "I want to——" The rest of his words died on a muffled oath, and there was a rumble of stones and a thud.

For a few seconds she continued to run. Then, aware of silence behind her, she stopped and turned. Nicolas was nowhere to be seen. Quickly her eyes moved over the uneven terrace. On the lower level, she saw a dark shadow where no shadow should have been. Horror gripped her as she realized what had happened. Anticipating that she intended to work her way back to the cottage, Nicolas had planned to intercept her on the terrace. Racing up them, he had not noticed where the steps were crumbling. He must have gone too near the edge and fallen.

She sped back across the grass to where he lay. In the faint light of a new moon, his face was a pale blur, though a dark line of blood oozed from a ragged cut on his temple. He was unconscious, and for a wild moment she thought he was dead. But then he stirred and groaned and tried to sit up.

"Don't move," she begged. "I'll fetch help."

He took no notice and sat up straight. "What happened?" he asked faintly.

"You fell. Do you think you can manage to get to the house, or should I get Eleanor to help you?"

Unsteadily, he got to his feet, but after a few steps he staggered, and she moved forward to take the weight of his body on hers. Her knees buckled at the pressure, and he pulled away and made an effort to walk unaided. But he was unable to do so, and he leaned on her again. Slowly they mounted the steps to the cottage.

In the living room, he slumped onto a chair, and Alex hurried into the kitchen to put on a kettle and then returned to the living room to pour him a brandy. As she did so, Eleanor came down the stairs. She was still dressed, and Alex realized it was not yet ten o'clock.

"I didn't expect you back so early." Eleanor's smile vanished as she caught sight of Nicolas.

"He fell on the steps," Alex said tersely. "Do you think we should call a doctor?"

"That won't be necessary." Nicolas spoke clearly for the first time. "All I need is a brandy."

Relieved that he sounded normal, Alex gave him the

glass, and he drained it at a gulp and handed it back to her.

"The cut on Nicolas's temple should be washed," Eleanor said.

Alex went into the kitchen and returned with a bowl of hot water and a clean towel.

Nicolas was lying on the settee with his eyes closed, but at her approach he opened them and looked at her. A bruise was already discoloring his temple, and there was a nasty gash where he had fallen and cut himself.

Carefully she removed the gravel, and, though she knew it must have been painful for him, he did not wince. By the time she had finished, the water in the bowl was stained red with his blood, and, looking at it, she felt sickened to know the accident had been her fault. She should have had the sense to realize he would not let her escape without hearing his side of the story that Elena had disclosed. Yet she had been afraid to listen to him because she had known how easily he could appease her anger. Because she desperately wanted to believe him, she would have forced herself to do so. It was this knowldge that had made her run away from him.

"I think you should see a doctor," she said shakily.

"I will call one when I get home." Nicolas stood up, swaying slightly.

"You're too ill to drive," Eleanor put in. "Perhaps you should stay here tonight."

"I don't want to put you out. I can—"

He stopped speaking and looked vague. His dark eyes met Alex's, but they did not focus properly, and even as she looked at them, they seemed to blur.

"I don't think I can drive," he said quietly and, without another word, sat down again and slumped into unconsciousness.

The suddenness with which he did so took both women by surprise, though Eleanor recovered first.

"It's an obvious case of concussion. We must get him to bed."

"We'll never be able to move him," Alex said. "I'll see if I can get the doctor."

Deploring the lack of a telephone, she ran from the cottage, praying that the doctor had not yet gone to bed. But even if he had, when he learned of the illustrious patient who needed him, he would surely come at once.

Her surmise was correct, and before she had finished her story, he was hurrying to his car, having the presence of mind to ask his son to come with them and to bring some pyjamas.

Some twenty minutes later, the doctor left the minute third bedroom where Nicolas, now conscious, lay.

"Do you think we should get him to hospital?" Alex asked as they went downstairs.

"I would prefer not to move him, but someone must stay with him throughout the night."

"That's no problem."

"Good. He seems to be rational, and his eyes are focusing properly. But if you notice any change in his condition, call me at once. In any event, I will be here early in the morning."

With a further word of reassurance to Eleanor, the doctor departed, and, refusing her godmother's offer to remain up with her, Alex sat down to her vigil by Nicolas's bed. He looked incongruous in young Jean's pyjamas, his broad shoulders straining at the material, his arms stretching several inches from below the sleeves. It was probably the first time he had ever worn cotton pyjamas. She was sure he had handmade silk ones with his monogram on the pocket.

"There's no need for you to stay with me," he said.

"I'll feel easier if I do."

"I won't." His eyes roamed over her. "In fact you're making me distinctly *un*easy!"

She smiled. "Don't talk so much, and go to sleep."

"We've *got* to talk. I want to——"

"Not tonight," she intercepted. "There'll be plenty of time tomorrow."

"You'll run away from me again."

"No I won't. I promise."

Satisfied by this, he settled back on the pillows and closed his eyes. A few moments later, his even breathing told her he was asleep, and she rose quickly and tiptoed forward to feast her eyes on him.

Nicolas. Her love. The only man who had meant anything to her. With a sigh she returned to her chair and fell into a light doze.

Nicolas's voice, speaking her name, jerked her into wakefulness, and she looked at him with apprehension.

"What's wrong? Do you feel ill?"

"No, I'm fine. Much better than I was." He raised his hand to his temple and the tape that covered one side of it. "I hope you feel suitably guilty?"

"Terribly so." Her eyes filled with tears. "I'm sorry, Nicolas."

"I'm the one who should be sorry. Sit close to me. We must talk."

"Let it wait till the morning." She repeated her earlier dictum. "It's better for you to sleep."

Once again he closed his eyes, but his fingers remained tightly curled around her own, and only when his breathing became even was she able to release her hand.

Several times during the night, she was roused by his muttering unintelligibly, but at dawn he relaxed into a quiet slumber, enabling her to do the same. It was eight o'clock when she awoke properly and, stretching her aching muscles, she tiptoed to the bed and looked at him. His face was flushed, and the bruise on his temple had darkened to purple. Stifling a sigh, she went down to the kitchen where Eleanor was already having breakfast.

"I peeped in to see you before I came down," her godmother said, "but you were asleep."

"Nicolas still is."

"Are you sure he isn't unconscious?"

"I don't think so. But now you mention it, I'll go and make sure." Quickly she went up to his room and, as she walked in, he turned his head on the pillow and looked at her with bright, knowing eyes.

"Good morning, Alex. I thought you'd deserted me."

"I'll never desert a man when he's down!" she smiled. "Would you like some coffee? Though on second thoughts, you'd better have tea."

"Just hot water with some lemon—and a razor." Her eyes dilated, and his mouth twitched. "I'm not contemplating suicide, Alex, I only want to shave!"

She smiled at her stupidity. "Don't you think you should rest until you've seen the doctor?"

"I have no intention of resting. I am going to get up." He went to swing his legs out of the bed and then stopped and lifted the counterpane. "I just want to make sure I'm wearing trousers!"

"You're wearing the doctor's son's pyjamas."

He eyed the stripes. "I'd hate to think these were *your* taste."

"I don't wear pyjamas."

"Indeed?" He looked at her with such interest that she stepped away from the bed.

"You *are* better, aren't you? I'll go and fetch your lemon and water."

When she returned with it, she was surprised to see him still in bed. But a quick glance at his clothes, which she had left in a tidy pile on a chair, showed her they were disarrayed, and she knew that in her absence he had tried—and failed—to get dressed.

"I suppose you felt giddy once you stood up?" she said without sympathy. "Don't you realize you've got concussion and have to rest?"

"I loathe staying in bed—by myself, that is."

"I'll buy you a teddy bear!"

He grinned. "My cuddly toy used to be a ship."

"A supertanker, no doubt!" She handed him the lemon juice. "I'm not sure whether I should give you anything to eat until the doctor has seen you."

"I don't want anything to eat, thanks."

He sipped the drink, and she watched him. Even unshaven, he was still incredibly handsome. His dark stubble accentuated the hard line of his cheek and jaw, giving him the saturnine look of a pirate an illusion heightened by his scarlet striped pyjamas.

"I still have to talk to you," Nicolas broke into her thoughts.

"Not now," she said quickly. "It isn't good for you to get agitated."

"I'll get more agitated if you don't let me say what I want."

The sound of a car coming down the lane prevented him from continuing, for a glance through the window told her it was Dr. Hugo. She went down to welcome him, then left him alone to examine Nicolas, only returning when he called for her to do so.

"Mr. Panos is much better," Dr. Hugo assured her. "But I would like him to stay in bed for a few more days."

"You can't get rid of me after all," Nicolas said cheerfully. "I need rest and an easy mind. Isn't that right, Doctor?"

"You certainly shouldn't have any excitement," the doctor agreed. "Rest and sleep and a light diet without any stimulants. I will be in to see you later today."

Declining Alex's offer of a coffee, he departed, and she looked suspiciously at Nicolas, wondering if he had deliberately encouraged the doctor to tell him he must stay here.

"Stop glaring at me and sit down," Nicolas said. "I have every intention of talking to you now."

Reluctantly, she perched on the edge of a chair but refused to look at him.

"I won't deny the truth of what Elena said last night," he began.

She turned in astonishment. "You mean you admit you set out to attract me?"

He nodded, wincing at the movement. "Don't forget that when I decided on what action to take, I based it on what Leon had told his mother about you. It was only when I met you for myself that I—but I go too fast." He levered himself into a higher position, wincing as he did so. "It isn't just my head that hurts," he muttered. "I ache all over. Now, where was I?"

"About to launch into an explanation that isn't necessary. I'm not angry with you, Nicolas. I don't blame you for not believing me when I say I don't want to marry Leon. After all, ninety-nine girls out of a hundred would jump at the chance of marrying into the Panos family."

"You aren't like any other girl," he said flatly. "That's why I fell in love with you. I originally came here to buy you off. I *won't* deny that. You aren't the first girl Leon's proposed to, and this wasn't the first time I'd had to bail him out."

"It doesn't say much for the love he feels for his fiancée. I assume it's an arranged match?"

"Leon agreed to it," Nicolas stated. "If he found he couldn't go through with it, he should have the courage to say so."

"But you knew he'd ask me to marry him. Didn't that tell you how he felt?"

"Leon frequently gets carried away by a pretty face. And yours is far more than that." He sighed. "Leon's love for you was genuine, but it lacked staying power. I told him this was the last time I was going to bail him out. Either he had to break his engagement and marry you—which would mean leaving the company and fending for himself—or else he had to go to Greece and set the date for his betrothal."

"You mean, he went willingly?"

"I'm afraid so. Panos security means more to him than anything else."

"Why didn't you tell me the truth before?" Alex's anger began to rise. "Were you afraid I might sue Leon for jilting me?"

"That *was* in my mind until I met you. As I said a moment ago, when I first came here, I only had his assessment of you to go on. Once I saw you for myself, I was afraid you were genuinely in love with him, and my main concern was to stop you being hurt."

"So you decided to make me fall in love with you instead?" she cried.

"Yes."

"And how was that going to help me?" Her voice rose. "Or hadn't you bothered to think that far ahead?"

"I've thought of nothing else!" he said with quiet vehemence. "My only concern is for your happiness. Our happiness. I have never felt for any woman the way I feel for you. I want to protect you . . . take care of you . . . stop anyone from hurting you. I wasn't sure about your feelings for Leon, and—"

"I kept telling you I didn't love him!"

"I wasn't sure you meant it. That's why I didn't tell you the truth about him. I wanted you to be in love with me first." He sighed heavily. "I was going to tell you the whole story last night, but Elena did it for me. And then you bolted."

"Because I was angry. I thought you were playing with me. I still do," she added and waited for him to deny it.

But he remained silent, and she glanced at the bed. He was lying back on the pillows, his eyes so narrow that she thought they were closed until he turned his head, and she saw the glint of jet.

"I love you," he whispered. "I love you and I want to spend my life with you."

What he said was not unexpected, though her reaction to it was. Yesterday evening, before his accident, she had been positive she could never have an affair with him, but now—having seen him unconscious and ill—she was not sure.

"Haven't you anything to say?" he asked.

"It wouldn't work," she whispered. "I'm not the type to be happy with that sort of life."

"What's wrong with it? Or are you merely finding an excuse because you don't love me? I won't believe you if you say that. You want me as much as I want you!" He stretched out his arms to her. "Darling, come close. Let me hold you."

"No." She shrank back in her chair. "Don't tempt me, Nicolas. Even if I said yes today, I'd regret it tomorrow."

"I won't let you regret it. I love you, and I'm going to marry you no matter how long I have to wait."

Shock held her motionless, and the blood seemed to solidify in her veins. Then it started to flow, coursing through her like a river flooding its banks. "Did you say *marry* you?"

"Yes. What else do you . . . . " His voice trailed away, and he jerked upright. "Did you think I was asking you to be my mistress? Is that why you said no?" He saw the answer in her face, and his own grew bleak. "You don't have much faith in my love, do you, Alex?"

"It has nothing to do with faith. You told me a Greek should marry a Greek. You said you didn't believe in mixed marriages—"

"I said that a marriage between people of different nationalities required an extra kind of love. The kind of love I have for you," he said deeply. "A love that won't let me find peace unless we spend the rest of our lives together."

Joy seeped through her, but still she remained aloof. "You're not well, Nicolas. Let's wait and talk about it again."

"My proposal isn't caused by concussion," he said humorously. "I nearly asked you to marry me the day I took you to the villa, but I was still unsure about you and Leon."

"I never loved him!" she cried. "Never." Stumbling forward, she knelt beside the bed. "It's been you almost from the beginning. That's why I was so sarcastic with you. You made me self-conscious . . . nervous of giving myself away." Her eyes filled with tears, and she buried her face against his arm. She felt his hand on her hair, stroking it rhythmically as though he were a father trying to pacify a child.

"I think I'll have some breakfast, after all." His voice was husky, and she looked up and saw the shine of sweat on his forehead.

"Poor darling," she whispered. "The doctor said no excitement, and here I am crying all over you!" Quickly, she rose. "I'll get you some breakfast at once."

"Do you think I can have a kiss first?"

Shyly she touched her lips to his. They were hot and

dry beneath her own and told her more easily than words that he was still far from well. "Close your eyes and rest," she pleaded. "I'll be back in a moment."

"We will have so *many* moments together," he murmured and, leaning his head on the pillows, obeyed her command.

Chapter Eight

To Alex's surprise, Eleanor was dismayed by Nicolas's proposal.

"After all, he only met you because he was determined to stop Leon from marrying you," she said, "and the reasons he gave still apply! You aren't Greek, and you haven't any money!"

"He doesn't need a dowry," Alex smiled, "and he doesn't care that I'm not Greek."

"His family will. Anyway, will you be able to live the same sort of life as the rest of his female relations?"

"What's wrong with the way they live? You talk as if they're kept in purdah!"

"Money makes its own purdah. You'll be cloistered and protected and watched over like a hawk. You might enjoy it for a few months—a few years, possibly—but eventually you'll get bored to death with idleness."

Her godmother's doubts raised all of her own, and Alex knew she would not have any peace until she had talked them over with Nicolas. But she was reluctant to say anything that might upset him, for Dr. Hugo still insisted he have maximum rest and quiet.

For two days, he stayed in his room and Alex went to the Post Office in Cabray and telephoned his villa to explain his absence. She spoke to a Greek man-servant but was not sure he believed her story. More likely he thought his master was off somewhere enjoying himself.

The idea made her smile, and she told Nicolas of it when he came down to the living room for the first time since his accident.

"The sooner we announce our engagement, the better," he said. "I hate the thought of people gossiping about you."

"And about *you*."

"I don't care for myself. You are the one I want to protect."

She was on the point of telling him about Eleanor's fears—and her own—when Jean, the doctor's son, arrived in his car.

"I asked Dr. Hugo if he could spare him to call for me," Nicolas explained as he saw Alex's surprise. "I have to make some telephone calls, and the doctor suggested I use his home in preference to the Post Office."

"I should think so, too. At least that way he can make sure you don't talk too long!"

Watching Nicolas being driven away, Alex was reminded of how little she knew of his life. He had never explained his work to her, and she was not sure whether this was because he felt she would not understand it or because he did not want her to know.

Whenever she had thought of marrying, she had assumed her husband would be in her own profession or one allied to it, which would have given them a kindred interest. But it was hard to feel interested in a shipping fleet no matter how lucrative it was, and the doubts Eleanor had raised in her rose higher still.

Sexual attraction alone was not a satisfactory basis for a lasting and happy marriage. There had to be other mutual interests, too. Yet Nicolas did not appear to think so. He was content to flirt with her and tease her and say all sorts of intimate things guaranteed to make her blush. But he was not willing to talk seriously with her on matters that he considered a man's province.

She did not know how far this attitude was due to indoctrination and the fact that the women in his life were only interested in trivia and how far to his own personal belief that the fair sex should be kept remote from everyday life and problems. All she did know was that she had no intention of leading the life of a sheltered butterfly.

"I wish you'd tell me about your business interests," she said to him late that afternoon as they lounged together on the lawn.

Because of his accident, they had closed the cottage to customers and had pinned a notice on the gate saying they would not be open until the repairs to the terrace had been completed. Alex was enjoying the enforced leisure, and Eleanor was spending the time putting the garden to rights.

"You'd find my work boring," Nicolas replied. "Keeping a shipping fleet busy is a matter of judging the political situation and knowing the right people at the right time."

"Have you ever been interested in politics as such?"

"My father brought me up to regard myself as a citizen of the world!"

"How farseeing of him!"

"His reasons were more financial than ideological!" Nicholas held out his hand to her. "Come and sit on my lap. You're too far away."

She came over and held out her hands to him, but when he reached for them his fingers missed hers.

"I must be suffering from double vision," he chuckled and, moving his hands again, pulled her onto his lap. *"Darling,"* he said huskily and pressed her against him.

She felt the stirring of his body and was too self-conscious to relax.

"You're not as emancipated as you would like me to believe," he whispered, gently rubbing his cheek along hers.

"I'm not emancipated at all."

"You are, compared with Greek girls. My sister went from the schoolroom to the bedroom."

The remark gave her the opening she wanted. "I'd have thought that was one reason you wouldn't want to marry me. You've been brought up to believe your wife will agree with everything you say and be content to live in a golden cage."

"I have no wish to marry a bird," he said humorously, "and I would be bored to death by a woman who agreed with me the whole time. You are all I have ever wanted, Alex. Now, lie close and let me hold you."

Still she held back. "I'm a foreigner, Nicolas, and you

gave that as one of your objections to Leon's marrying me. Surely it applies to you too?"

"I have already told you the answer to that," he said forcefully. "I am a stronger character than my cousin. He needs the right marriage in order to make sure he always does the right thing. Whereas I—"

"Do the right thing all the time!"

"Exactly!"

He caught her close and pressed his lips to the nape of her neck. His touch sent a shiver down her spine and made it difficult for her to think of anything except his closeness.

"Stop worrying about foolish things, my golden sweetheart. The past is finished, and what you and I were no longer counts. It's what we'll be together that matters."

It was an eminently satisfactory reply, and she responded to it by winding her arms 'round his neck. They remained like this for a long while, and his willingness to hold her without making love to her told her more clearly than words that he had not yet recovered his health. She had read somewhere that concussion often had a delayed reaction, and she wondered if he should see a specialist. She would ask Dr. Hugo when he called tomorrow.

However her disquiet grew appreciably that evening when Nicolas complained of a headache and then looked at his watch.

"I really shouldn't stay here another night. I've a dozen servants at the villa doing nothing except eat their heads off! I think I'll drive back."

"In the dark and at this hour?" Eleanor expostulated.

"I was hoping Alex would come with me and spend the night at my home."

"If you wanted to leave, we should have gone earlier," Alex said.

"Or asked my chauffeur to come and collect me," he sighed. "I don't know why I didn't think of it. That blow on the head must have affected me."

"Perhaps deep down you wanted to stay here," Eleanor countered. "For you, it must be like playing truant."

His smile showed appreciation of her remark. "I do feel as if I've opted out of the world of commerce. It's hours since I spoke business."

"You made masses of calls from Dr. Hugo's," Alex reminded him. "He said you talked to New York and Venezuela and were twenty minutes on a call to Tokyo! I think he was rather impressed with your worldwide connections!"

A smile lifted the corners of Nicolas's mouth, drawing her attention to his sensual lower lip. "My father is in Japan at the moment, and I wanted to tell him about us."

"So soon?" She could not hide her surprise, and he frowned.

"Why not? I want to marry you as soon as possible, and it is necessary for my father to be present."

Happiness gave Alex a buoyancy that made her feel she was floating. "Was your father surprised?"

"Naturally." He waited as though expecting another question and, when it did not come, his smile grew tight. "Say it, Alex. I insist that you bring it into the open."

"Bring what into the open?"

"Your fears." He set down his fork. His meal, she

noticed, was almost untouched, and he looked at her with intensity. "Your fears that my father will not wish me to marry an ex-girlfriend of Leon's."

"I was *never* Leon's girlfriend!" she insisted.

"And also whether he objected because you aren't Greek," Nicolas continued remorselessly. "But he did neither. He has confidence in the way he brought me up and is prepared to rely on my judgment. All he wants is to meet you and see for himself how exquisite you are."

It seemed too good to be true that Christoff Panos would so easily accept an English wife for his only son. But to say this would make Nicolas angry, and she was unwilling to excite him further. Already she was worried by the flush on his cheeks, and she debated whether to ask Dr. Hugo to come and see him again tonight. But when she suggested it, Nicolas laughed and shook his head.

"I feel fine. I'm flushed only because I keep thinking of my future with you."

But she was still not reassured, particularly when he pushed aside his plate and stood up.

"I will go upstairs and rest. Those telephone calls have made me tired."

"Would you like me to bring you a hot drink?" she asked.

"I will be in the Land of Nod before you have even made it!"

Lightly touching her cheek, he left the kitchen, and Eleanor leaned her hands on the pine table and looked at Alex.

"I'm worried about him. If he's no better in the

morning, we must arrange for him to go home and see his own doctor."

"Perhaps he was worried by his call to his father. I don't believe Mr. Panos was as sanguine about me as Nicolas says."

"You could be right." Eleanor began to clear the table. "That's why I don't want you to build up your hopes. Nicolas might still be persuaded to change his mind."

"You speak as if you don't like him."

"I like him very much. But I'm still not sure you're right for each other. Don't rush into marriage, Alex. Once you're his wife, you won't have any life of your own."

"My life will be with him—which is what I want."

"Won't you mind giving up your acting?"

"It looks as if acting has given *me* up," Alex said ruefully. "I'll miss not having had the chance to prove my ability, but not deeply enough to let it worry me."

"So you'll be content to live like a lap dog?"

Alex tossed her head. "Stop exaggerating the facts, godmother of mine. I assure you I'll be perfectly happy to make a home for Nicolas and have his children."

Murmuring that she knew when she was beaten, Eleanor started to wash the dishes.

It was after ten when they went to bed. Alex undressed and sat by the window, staring out at the moonlight-drenched countryside and wondering what the future held for her. There were many barriers to be surmounted, and not the least of them was her future father-in-law.

And what of Leon? How would he react when he learned she was going to marry his cousin?

Tightening the belt of her housecoat, she went across the small landing and listened outside Nicolas's door. All was quiet, and she was turning away when she heard him call her name. It was soft yet distinct, and she paused, wondering if he were dreaming. Then he called her again, louder, and she opened the door and stepped inside.

He was sitting up in bed, and she hurried over to him. Only as he caught her arm and she felt the heat of his hand did she realize he had a high temperature.

"Stay with me, Alex."

"Of course. Do you feel ill?"

"I'm thirsty."

"I'll get you a drink."

"Don't leave me."

"I'll only be a moment."

Gently, she disengaged her hand and tiptoed down to the kitchen to make him a glass of warm fruit juice. She wondered whether to lace it with brandy and then decided against it. If they were on the telephone, she would have called Dr. Hugo. It was ridiculous to live in such an isolated part of the countryside and not have the benefit of instant communication. Regardless of the cost, she was going to install a phone for Eleanor.

Careful not to make any noise, she went back upstairs, stopping on the way to get a bottle of aspirins from the bathroom. Nicolas was lying down, but he sat up when he saw her. His pyjama jacket was drenched with sweat, and she took it off and rubbed his shoulders dry with a towel. He had a wonderful physique, and she was intensely aware of the bronze sheen of his skin and the soft tangle of dark hairs on his chest. Muscles rippled across his shoulders, and she longed to press her lips to them. But there would be time for loving. Right now he needed aspirins more than passion.

But Nicolas seemed to think the exact opposite, and as she handed him another pyjama jacket, he pulled her down onto the bed.

"You mustn't leave me," he said loudly.

"I'll stay until you've had your drink."

She held herself away from him but was not proof against his strength as he pulled her close and pressed his mouth upon hers. "I love you," he said huskily. "I can't think of anything except how much I want you."

She went to turn her head away from him, but he twined his fingers through her thick gold hair and clasped her head so firmly that she was powerless to avoid his kisses. Not that she wanted to avoid them, for there was a demand in them to which she responded. It was only as his kisses deepened and she felt the penetration of his tongue that she realized the danger of her position and became afraid. She was alone in Nicolas's room, both of them in a state of semiundress, and it would take little to send the barrier of control crashing between them.

"Nicolas, don't," she pleaded and tried to struggle free.

"I want you," he muttered and, pulling her down beside him, twisted his body and was instantly on top of her.

"Nicolas, you mustn't! Let me go. Please let me go."

Ignoring her cries, he buried his head between her breasts, kissing the shaded hollow between them before letting his mouth travel over the swelling curves. His touch aroused her to a fever of passion she had never before known, and she was filled with a desire so strong that it overwhelmed her common sense. Unable to stop herself, she stroked his shoulders and ran her hands down his back. The feathery movement of her fingers was his final undoing, and with a groan he sought her mouth again, parting her lips in a kiss of tantalizing intimacy. Masterfully, his tongue rubbed hers, making it impossible for her to give him anything other than the answering response he wanted. His arms gathered her closer, and the whole length of his body pressed upon hers.

She tried to shift away by burrowing deeper into the bed, but the movement only served to increase their closeness, for one of his legs came between hers and forced them apart. Her fear increased, and with all her strength she pushed against him. But nothing could lift his weight, and she again tried to twist her head away from his kisses, hoping that if she could do so, he would return to his senses.

But the more she struggled, the more persistent he became, and his arms seemed like steel bands around her. No longer was there any gentleness in his hold. He was a man afire with his own need, enflamed by a desire that burned away all social pretence, leaving only the rawness of a passion bent on assuagement.

"Nicolas, don't! You're hurting me." But her pleading had no chance to be voiced, for his mouth was cruelly covering hers, silencing all sound except his heavy breathing and her own lighter, panting sighs.

Unexpectedly, he lifted his head away from her and looked deep into her eyes. "You're mine, Alex. I won't let you go."

Giving her no time to reply, he started to kiss her again, more gently this time but still with inexorable persistence. Now his hands were persistent too, no longer clasping her back but caressing her body. Her dressing gown had long since been torn open, and her flimsy nightdress was a wisp of soft chiffon that presented no barrier between their two bodies as his fingers stroked the curve of her waist and hips.

The wild throbbing of his body awakened an equally wild throbbing in hers. It had been difficult enough to fight him before, but now she was having to fight herself as well, and the urge to do so was lessening as her desire rose beneath the skilled mastery of his touch. No longer were they two different people but two halves of a whole, striving for unity, seeking that moment of indivisible communion when ecstasy reaches its height and spirit touches spirit.

"Nicolas!"

She gave a high convulsive cry and was lost, carried away by a storm of passion that grew more and more frenzied until, released in a final tumultuous torrent, it left her as exhausted as a swimmer emerging from a gale-tossed sea onto a tranquil shore.

For a long while, she lay motionless, her body bruised from Nicolas's onslaught. As a teenaged girl, she had often thought about love and physical union, giggling with her friends at descriptive passages in the various forbidden novels they had all read. As she grew older, her romantic view of sex became a more realistic one, though in the back of her mind there had remained a picture of the conquering hero who would one day sweep her into his arms and show her a world of undreamed delight.

As Nicolas had done tonight.

Yet she had been taken unawares, forced into a surrender against her will. She knew she should be angry, but, with her body still weak from surrender, she could only feel love and tenderness for him—the same tenderness with which, a few moments ago, they had lain together like children, caressed and caressing, kissed and kissing, as if, having fulfilled their love, they could now spare time to be loving. It was those moments of gentleness that had washed away any re-crimination she might have flung at him, though she could not dispel her surprise at his unexpected lack of control.

She raised herself on one elbow, the better to look at him. He was lying with his eyes closed, and, in the glow of the bedside lamp, his tan seemed deeper. A gentle touch on his forehead told her that his increased color came from the heat raging within him. Was this the reason for his inexplicable behavior? Could his fever have burned away his self-control and turned him into a primitive man eschewing all social conven-tion? It was a logical explanation—so logical that she knew it to be true. In normal circumstances, Nicolas was not the man to force himself upon a woman no matter how much he desired her. And when love was added to desire, he was even less likely to do so.

Gently, she stood up. Her nightdress fell limply around her, and she shivered and reached to where her dressing gown lay on the floor. As she straightened and looked at Nicolas again she saw that his eyes were open. They were bright as burning coals, and, like coal, they seemed to glow red as they caught the lamp-light.

"Christ! I'm hot. It's like a furnace in here. Open

the window." His voice was jerky, and he sat up and threw off the bedclothes.

"Nicolas, don't, you'll catch cold." She picked up his pyjama jacket and draped it around his shoulders. "Darling, put this on."

"No, I'm too hot." He threw the jacket away. "My head is on fire."

She picked up the aspirins from the table together with the hot orange juice, which had now grown tepid. It seemed a lifetime ago that she had made it, yet it could not have been more than an hour—an hour that had changed her life, turning her from a virgin into a woman. Her cheeks burned, and she glanced away from Nicolas.

"My head is exploding," he muttered, and quickly she turned to him again, losing her embarrassment as she experienced his pain. A short while ago, he had had a man's need of her; now he needed her as a child did, and she longed to cradle him in her arms and comfort him.

"Take these aspirins, darling. They will help to bring down your temperature."

He looked at her blankly, and she was not sure if he had heard her or did not understand what she had said. She shook two aspirins out of the bottle and handed them to him. He looked at them blankly and she raised his hand to his lips and made him put them in his mouth.

"Swallow the tablets with some orange juice," she ordered, and was relieved when he did so without demur. "Put on your pyjama jacket, too, or you'll get a chill."

He did so, then pointed jerkily to the window. "Open it. I can't stand the heat."

"You will feel cooler if you stop thrashing around. Lie down and close your eyes."

"It makes my head worse." His face contorted. "What's happened to me? Where am I? And where's Demetrius? *He* should be here with me, not you."

She stared at him. "Your valet is at the villa."

"I know that," he said irritably. "Send him up to me at once."

Enlightenment dawned, and, as it did, her fear increased. Nicolas thought he was in his own home. That was why he believed Demetrius was within call.

"You aren't at the villa," she said gently. "You're staying with me at Cabray."

"Why?"

His words confirmed her fears, and with an effort she controlled her anxiety. "You had a slight accident and are staying with me for a few days. Don't you remember?"

"No." He closed his eyes, and she remained beside the bed, waiting to see what he did. But he seemed to have fallen into instant slumber, and she crossed to a chair and sat down, unwilling to leave him alone.

Nicolas slept restlessly, tossing and turning on the pillows and moving his head as though looking for some place where he could rest in comfort. From time to time, he spoke in Greek, though she was able to decipher her own name and Leon's, as well as his father's, which he repeated several times.

All at once he gave a loud cry and jumped half out of bed. "I've got to see my father! Karamis is trying to double-cross us."

"Nicolas, please, you can't go anywhere. It's the middle of the night!"

She struggled to keep him seated on the bed, but he pushed her away, and she was wondering how to cope with him when the door opened and Eleanor came in. A quick glance at the scene, and she hurried to the bed and gripped Nicolas with firm hands.

"He's delirious," she said to Alex. "How long has he been like this?"

"A few hours. I've a feeling it was coming on when he went to bed."

"How long have you been with him?" Eleanor's glance took in Alex's disheveled appearance.

"He called out and said he wanted a drink. I fetched it for him, and he—he wouldn't let me leave him."

She looked at Nicolas, who was lying back against the pillows, as docile as a child. His eyes were wide open, but when she bent forward they did not focus on her.

"He doesn't know I'm here," she whispered agitatedly. "Do you think we should call Dr. Hugo?"

Eleanor glanced out of the window at the dark sky. "Let's wait a couple of hours. Nicolas might be better once his temperature goes down."

"You go back to bed," Alex said. "There's no point both of us losing a night's sleep."

Eleanor nodded and went out, and Alex settled in a chair. Nicolas was still quiet, and she hoped the aspirins were beginning to work. Fitfully she dozed, one ear alert in case he called her, but there was no sound from him, and she was the first one to awaken properly.

It was a lovely summer morning, and she felt an uplift of her spirits, as though the bright new day was heralding a bright new life. And it was, she assured herself: her life with Nicolas. She tiptoed to the bed and stared down at him. He was sleeping as peacefully as a child and looked far less than his age. His mouth, normally tight and controlled, was curved in a half smile, and the hard line of his cheek had a softer edge to it. She drew away from the bed, and, as she did so, his blue-shadowed lids lifted, and his eyes stared directly into hers. They were no longer bright with fever but opaque with slumber, and as she watched them, they became clear and lucid.

"Alex," he murmured and lifted his hand towards her.

"Lie still and try and sleep again," she whispered. "It's barely six o'clock."

His beautifully shaped brows, dark as his hair, drew together. "Why are you here? Why aren't you in bed?"

"You weren't well, and I—I thought it better if I stayed with you."

Hearing this, he sat up, and the sureness of his movements told her he was considerably improved. "You mean you've been here all night?"

"Yes."

"Did I call for you?"

She nodded. "Don't you remember?"

"I remember saying goodnight to you downstairs and coming to my room. After that, everything is blank."

There was an emptiness in her stomach that seemed to make itself felt in the hollowness of her voice. "Don't you remember *anything*?"

"Only what I just said. Why? Did I make an awful racket during the night?"

"No," she said quickly. "You weren't too noisy. You were delirious, and I stayed here to quiet you."

"What a pity I was off my head," he said ruefully. "This is the second time I've had you in my room all night without doing anything about it!"

Helplessly, she stared at him, wondering whether to tell him what had happened. She had no experience of how to deal with someone suffering from concussion and was not sure if the shock of learning the truth might cause a relapse. Because of her uncertainty, she kept silent.

"You'd better go to your room and rest." He was speaking again. "You look as pale as a ghost."

"Blondes always look washed-out in the morning," she said lightly.

"I don't believe *you* do."

He drew her hand to his lips. The gentleness of his action was in marked contrast to the rough way he had pulled her onto his bed the night before, and this, more than anything else he could have done, highlighted the difference between Nicolas with a fever and Nicolas in command of himself.

"You aren't a wishy-washy blonde, my beautiful Alex," he whispered. "You're a blonde as golden as Hymettus honey and twice as fragrant." The tip of his tongue rubbed against her palm. "You taste delicious, too, but you'd better go while I still have the strength to send you!"

The longing to tell him that a short while ago he had done exactly the opposite was so strong in her that she was able to keep silent only by swinging away from the bed and half running to the door.

"Don't be frightened of me," he teased: "It was the Norsemen who raped the fair Saxon women, not the dark and passionate Greeks!"

Scarlet-faced, she closed the door behind her, then leaned on it as she fought for self-control. It was incredible that Nicolas had no recollection of last night, that he could look at her without any remembrance of the passion that had flared between them.

Dejectedly, she went to her room and lay on the bed. She would rest for an hour and then go to Dr. Hugo. Though Nicolas was considerably better, it would be advisable to tell the doctor of his delirium. She closed her eyes and slept.

Chapter Nine

Dr. Hugo came to see Nicolas immediately he learned of his delirium and, after some deliberation, advised him to go to a private clinic in Nice for a complete examination.

"Why the fuss?" Nicolas asked. "I'm fine today."

"In cases of concussion, it is better to be safe than sorry."

"You mean I might lose my memory again?"

"Possibly."

"Don't worry, my darling," Nicolas grinned at Alex, "I still remember I asked you to marry me!"

"But you remember nothing of what happened last night?" Dr. Hugo was in no way appeased by his patient's lighthearted attitude.

"Not a single thing." Nicolas was still amused. "I'm

sure I would remember if anything important had happened. You're worrying needlessly, doctor."

"Nevertheless, I will drive you to the clinic myself. But first I will call your own doctor and arrange to meet him there."

Tentatively, Alex offered to accompany Nicolas to Nice, but he refused to let her, saying firmly that two doctors fussing over him were more than enough, without also having an overanxious girl.

"If I were a bank clerk, old Hugo would have had me at work again within twenty-four hours," he concluded. "It's only because I'm Nicolas Panos that he's making all this fuss."

"One has to protect the heir to such a vast fortune," she teased and was roughly pulled into his arms.

"Is that how you see me?" he demanded.

"Of course. Don't you know I only love you for your money?"

Black eyes stared into grey ones, and, seeing the expression in the darker pair, the grey ones darkened, too.

"You don't believe I mean it, do you?" she whispered. "I'd love you if you really were a bank clerk. In fact, I wish you were."

"How dull I would be!"

"At least you wouldn't doubt me."

"I don't doubt you," he said huskily. "I only doubt my luck in having captured you. I won't have any peace until you're my wife."

She longed to cry that she was already his wife but bit back the words, knowing that if she said them, she would have to explain much more that he should not know in his present condition.

Watching him being driven away later that morning, she felt as though a chapter in her life had ended. Nicolas's chauffeur would be coming to collect his car later that day and would take her down to the coast. Meanwhile, all she could do was to wait and hope that the examination in the clinic would not disclose anything seriously wrong with him.

"Will you be staying at the villa with Nicolas?" Eleanor asked during lunch, which they ate on the terrace in the one corner that was still safe for walking.

"I don't know. He didn't say anything about it, but I'll go prepared just in case he asks me to stay."

"Don't take too much for granted," the older woman said slowly.

"You mean he may regret the proposal when he recovers his senses?"

"You know very well what I mean. Out here," Eleanor waved her arm at the tranquil scene, "it's easy to forget one's family and tradition and think only in terms of the idyllic today."

"Nicolas is also thinking of the idyllic tomorrow," Alex retorted. "But don't worry. If he starts to look anxious, I'll give him every opportunity to tell me he's changed his mind."

"If he does, it won't ruin your whole life," Eleanor said soberly. "You've known him only a month."

"But I do know him," Alex said quietly. "In every sense of the word."

There was something in her tone that made Eleanor stare at her. "You don't mean . . . ? You and Nicolas haven't . . . ?"

"We have." Alex clenched her hands. "Last night."

"*Last night?* Oh my dear, I wish you hadn't."

"It wasn't the way it seems." Alex pushed back her chair and went to stand by the balustrade. "I fought him, Eleanor. I fought him as hard as I could."

"You mean he took you by force? Of all the—"

"He didn't know!" Alex interrupted, swinging round. "He was delirious. Out of his mind!"

Various expressions passed over Eleanor's face: doubt, astonishment, and finally compassion. "How dreadful for you. Why didn't you call me?"

"I didn't have much chance. Nicolas is strong, and . . . . " Alex returned to the table. "I couldn't believe it was happening. It was like a nightmare."

Eleanor shook her head. "What did he say this morning, when he realized what had happened?"

"He *doesn't* realize it," Alex said. "He remembers saying goodnight to us down here, but after that his mind is a blank."

"But you've told him, haven't you?"

"No. I thought it would be too much of a shock. Dr. Hugo said he shouldn't be worried or have any excitement." Alex rested her head in her hands. "It wouldn't make him feel good to know he practically raped me."

"There's no 'practically' about it," Eleanor sniffed. "He did."

"Without knowing it." Alex flung out her hands. "That's the only reason I haven't told him. I'll wait till he's better."

Eleanor sighed and patted Alex's arm. "No wonder you looked like death this morning. It must have been a heartbreaking experience for you."

Alex relaxed in the warmth of her godmother's understanding, carried back to her childhood, when she had always been able to turn to Eleanor for comfort.

"It hasn't made me hate him," she whispered. "It's made me realize how much I love him. . . . I know I can never belong in the same way to anyone else."

"He doesn't have an exclusive on it!" Eleanor retorted.

Alex smiled, and so did Eleanor. Then suddenly they were both giggling like schoolgirls, using humor as a release from tension.

When Alex next saw Nicolas he was in a large corner bedroom of the most exclusive private clinic on the Côte d'Azur. His bed was littered with documents and letters, and, as she came in, a male secretary gathered them together and went to the door, murmuring in Greek as he did so.

"Stephanos!" Nicolas called him back. "Before you go, I would like you to meet my fiancée."

The man bowed in Alex's direction. "I was delighted at the news," he murmured.

She smiled her thanks and was relieved when he closed the door behind him. Then she ran across to the bed, arms outstretched.

Nicolas caught her close, only releasing her when she protested she was getting a crick in her neck.

"You shouldn't bend over the bed," he teased. "You should lie on it. It is easier for making love."

She blushed. "Nicolas, don't."

"I can't," he said whimsically. "Not while I'm here!"

"Why *are* you here?" she said anxiously. "I thought you would be at home."

"They want to do a few more tests on me. Nothing serious. Just to make sure I haven't had a slight hemorrhage." She went so white that he gripped her hand. "Darling, it's nothing. I feel as fit as a flea. As I said this morning, if it weren't for who I am, the medics wouldn't even be looking at me."

Alex pretended to be reassured, but she was far from easy in her mind, and, leaving him on the pretext that she wanted to have a snack, she asked the matron for the name of Nicolas's personal doctor and telephoned to make an immediate appointment to see him.

Dr. Margrave was far more illustrious in his profession than Dr. Hugo, and Alex knew she would have received short shrift from him had she not been Nicolas's fiancée. As it was, he was affable and informative.

"Mr. Panos had a slight hemorrhage," he informed her, "and must take things easy for a few weeks. He must give his body time to repair the damage."

"What damage?"

"A brain hemorrhage can cause a clot. This either dissolves of its own accord or may necessitate treatment. However, I hope that in a few weeks all will be well."

"And if it isn't?"

"Let us reserve our pessimism for when it's required. I am sure all will be well. The most important thing is for Mr. Panos to rest and have no excitement."

"He was working with his secretary when I saw him this afternoon."

"So the matron informed me. I have now given her strict instructions what to do. And Mr. Panos has already forbidden the secretary to go to the Clinic." Seeing Alex's perplexity, he added: "Mr. Christoff Panos."

"I thought he was in Japan?"

"He returned this afternoon."

The doctor was not successful in hiding his surprise

that Alex had not known of her future father-in-law's arrival.

"I haven't met him yet," Alex said frankly. "Nicolas and I only became engaged a few days ago."

"Then you should be able to see he obeys you! It is imperative for him to have complete rest and no excitement."

Alex bit her lip. It was difficult to misunderstand the doctor's order, yet she had to clarify it in her own mind. "I have to—to tell my fiancé something important," she said carefully. "It might upset him—not because it's bad news but because it will make him angry with himself—and I wonder if—"

"For the moment, he must have no stress whatever," Dr. Margrave interrupted. "In a few weeks' time you may tell him what you wish. But not now."

Leaving him, Alex returned to the Clinic, anxious in case her long absence had made Nicolas suspicious. Since she could not tell what had happened last night, she determined to put it from her mind until she could speak of it. Indeed, the more she thought it over, the more inclined she was never to tell him. Nicolas had great pride, and to learn he had taken her by force might make him feel such repugnance for himself that it could affect their relationship. Yes, perhaps silence was the best solution not only for a few weeks but forever.

With this decision made, she experienced a sensation of release and lightheartedly ran along the corridor to Nicolas's room, knocking and entering it without waiting for him to reply.

At once she drew back, disconcerted to find that he was not alone. An elderly man was with him: a man whose looks proclaimed him to be Christoff Panos. Annoyed for not having realized he might be here, Alex wished she had been wearing something smarter than a blue denim dress and jacket. What a far cry she must look from the rich Greek heiress he had envisaged for his son!

"So you are Alex." Mr. Panos's voice had the same depth as his son's but was more heavily accented. "I was preparing myself to offer my congratulations, but now I see I must give them to Nico."

He strode over and enveloped her in a bearlike embrace; a big, broad-shouldered man who looked—Alex knew—the way Nicolas would look in thirty years' time.

Mr. Panos drew back from her but still kept his hands on her shoulders as he drew her towards the bed. "Well Nico, have you set the wedding date?"

"There would be no point without consulting you first," his son replied. "I wanted to be sure it wouldn't clash with the launching of one of our tankers!"

His father chuckled. "A tanker would rate a poor second when it comes to your wedding. I have waited a long time for that day, Nico, and nine months after it, I hope for an even better event!"

Alex blushed and was aware of both men admiring her color. Mr. Panos spoke in Greek to Nicolas, who replied in the same tongue, and then in English to Alex.

"Don't let my father embarrass you, darling. I've just told him we haven't discussed the question of children and when we do, our decision about them will be our own affair."

"Decide what you like," Christoff Panos grunted, "but make it five children at least." He looked sheepishly at Alex. "Four, maybe. It is a good round number!"

It was impossible for Alex to remain embarrassed in the face of such genuine longing. Besides, there was a boyish quality about Mr. Panos that made it hard not to warm to him. Only his habit of breaking into Greek disconcerted her, and she made up her mind to start learning the language as soon as possible. It was the only way of keeping up with this volatile family.

Mentioning her decision when she was alone with Nicolas a little later, her future father-in-law having displayed unusual tact in departing, he expressed his delight that she wanted to learn his language.

"If you speak Greek, it will be easier when I make love to you," he whispered, raising her hand and kissing her fingers. "There are many poetic phrases that cannot be successfully translated into English."

She tried to remember the things he had said to her the night before. Was it only last night? So much had happened today that she felt she had already lived a lifetime since that overwhelming experience.

She glanced at her wristwatch and stood up. "You're supposed to rest and have no excitement. I can see I'll have to talk to your father about it."

"He has already forbidden all visitors to come here," Nicolas grinned. "Only my family—and that means Papa and you." He hesitated. "And Leon and his mother, of course."

"Of course." Alex hoped her voice was natural. "They are your family, and I would expect them to come and see you. Is Leon back from Greece?"

"Not yet. How will you feel about seeing him?"

She looked at Nicolas, too hurt to be angry. "I love *you*. Why do you need constant reassurance?"

"I never have until now. But with you, I'm like a callow youth in love for the first time. I can't believe you should love me in return." He pressed her hand to his lips again. "We will be married as soon as I get out of here."

"No lavish wedding?" she teased.

"Is that what you want? Say the word, and you shall have it. A hundred guests or a thousand? And shall it be at the villa or in New York or London?"

"Nico, please!" Laughing, she rested her cheek upon his. "I only want *you*. I don't care where we get married as long as we're together." She drew away from him and placed a swift kiss on his mouth before moving back from the bed. "No excitement," she warned him.

"You won't always get your own way," he grumbled.

"Then I'll take advantage of it while I can." Blowing him a kiss from the door, she went out.

Only as she emerged from the Clinic did she realize she had forgotten to ask Nicolas if he had made arrangements for her to stay at his villa, and she knew a sense of surprise that he had not thought to mention it himself. Or had he taken it for granted she would stay there?

"Alex!" a deep voice called, and she saw a royal blue limousine slowly moving alongside her.

"Mr. Panos!" she exclaimed.

"Whom else did you expect?" He opened the door and beckoned her in. "You have been a long time saying good-bye to Nico," he growled good-naturedly. "I have been waiting to take you home." The car moved forward, and the old man swiveled 'round to look at her. "I promised my son I would take care of you. He was worried in case you would find it lonely at the villa without him."

Tears filled her eyes at Nicolas's solicitude, and she was angry with herself for having doubted him.

"Nico can be thoughtful," Mr. Panos said as if divining her thoughts, "though it isn't an emotion that women have usually brought out in him. But then, you are the only one he has wanted to marry." A big hand came out to touch her cheek. "You must tell me about yourself."

"What would you like to know?" Alex asked.

"Everything. But wait until we get home. It is better if we talk over dinner."

"I went out for a snack," she said, remembering she had told this to Nicolas.

"No, you didn't," Mr. Panos replied. "I have just spoken to Dr. Margrave, and he told me you had been to see him."

She reddened. "I'm sorry. You are right. I wanted to find out for myself how ill Nicolas was. I wouldn't have spoken to the doctor if I had known you were here."

"Why not? You are my son's fiancée, and in Greek eyes you are as good as married to him." He looked at her keenly. "We Greeks have a solid belief in the unity of the family. When you marry one Panos, you marry them all!"

"What a frightening thought!"

"Is it I who frighten you or my nephew Leon?"

Though she had already had a glimpse of Mr. Panos's candor, she was taken aback by this particular display of it. "I don't know what Nicolas has told you about Leon and myself," she said slowly, "but I never loved him and I repeatedly told him so."

"Leon believes what he wants to believe."

"So it seems. But *I* am speaking the truth."

"I know." A hand rested on hers. "We will not talk of Leon any more."

"Nicolas still doubts me," she blurted out.

"Because he is in love with you, and love can cloud a man's judgment. Once you are his wife, he will come to his senses."

They arrived at the villa, and Alex was shown into a bedroom facing the sea. It was luxuriously furnished with cornflower-blue carpeting underfoot and white silk curtains at the tall windows. Was this the room she would share with Nicolas when they were married, or would they have separate bedrooms? She wished she knew more about the intimacies of his life and marveled that there was so much more about him she still did not know.

When she went downstairs a quarter of an hour later, Mr. Panos was hovering in the hall as if waiting for her, and he escorted her to the terrace where a flower-decked glass table was set for dinner. As one beautifully prepared course followed another, he encouraged her to talk about herself, which she did with determined frankness, a fact that he commented upon.

"Thank you for your openness, my dear. Now at least I feel as if I know you."

Only then did Alex hesitate, longing to ask the question uppermost in her mind, yet oddly reluctant to do so. But in the end her curiosity won. "Why don't you object to me, Mr. Panos? I can't be the sort of girl you wanted your son to marry."

For a long moment there was silence, and she was not sure if he was weighing his words or debating whether to be honest. But when he spoke, she knew that honesty had won.

"When Nico was a baby I thought in terms of a Greek heiress. The daughter of one of my friends, perhaps, or of another shipping tycoon. But as he grew older, I realized he would make his own choice. After all, it was I who had taught him to be independent—and all I could do then was to pray he would not fall for beauty alone but would have the sense to look for intelligence and integrity too. As he *has* done."

Tears filled Alex's eyes, and, seeing their glitter, Mr. Panos stood up. "To bed, my child. You are tired."

"I've had a trying few days," she confessed, "and I'm still worried about Nicolas."

"So am I." The broad shoulders lifted. "Men like myself tend to think of the power of money," he went on, "and it takes an accident like Nico's to make one see how unimportant it is."

Alex remembered this as she lay in bed listening to the sound of the surf breaking on the rocks far below. But it was on a final thought of Nicolas and how much she loved him that she finally fell asleep.

Chapter Ten

A few days later, Alex returned to Cabray to collect some more of her clothes.

"Nicolas wants me to stay at the villa with his father," she explained to Eleanor, "and he'd like you to come and stay there, too."

"I'm your godmother, Alex. I have no intention of playing mother-in-law!"

Nothing Alex could say would make Eleanor change her mind, though she did promise to have dinner at the villa one evening during the week.

"Tell me when, and I'll send the chauffeur for you."

"Make sure the car is this year's model!"

Alex laughed. "You see how easily I'm being corrupted by luxury!"

"Not you," Eleanor said staunchly, "but you can corrupt *me* by driving me into the village. There's

159

nothing better than a chauffeur for elevating my status with the Cabray shopkeepers!"

Leaving her godmother entering the butcher's shop, Alex herself was driven back to the coast and went directly to the Clinic.

She arrived there in time to join Christoff Panos, who was talking to Dr. Margrave.

"I don't understand why your son's improvement is so slow," the doctor confessed. "It may be Nature's way of saying that the body requires a complete rest. Mr. Panos has been working at fever pitch for years, and when the nervous system unexpectedly receives a shock, it can often cause a total collapse."

"Not in Nico's case," Christoff Panos replied. "He enjoys every single moment of his work. If he isn't making progress, there's a reason for it, and we must find out what. Is there anyone else we can call in to examine him?"

"He's already seen Sir Matthew Danvers, and Danvers agrees with the treatment he's having."

"So be it, then. All we can do is wait and see." The old man put his arm across Alex's shoulder. "Go up and stay with Nico, my child. He is anxious to see you."

Alex did as she was told. As always when she saw Nicolas, she found it hard to believe he was ill, for his skin glowed with health and his eyes shone with vitality. Yet the vitality never lasted, and after a brief chat, he was content to lie back on his pillows and let her and his father do the talking, occasionally interpolating a remark to show he was listening. It was this quick failing of energy that worried Alex more than anything else, and though she could not deny the fame of the neurologist who had flown from England to see him, she wondered if there was something he had failed to diagnose.

Driving back to the villa that evening, she voiced her fears to Nicolas's father.

"I'm inclined to agree with you," he said. "Even the best men can make a mistake. If Nico is no better by the end of the week, I will ask Darrell Dexter to see him."

It was a name Alex had read about only a month ago, when *Paris-Match* had written a long article about Dexter's pioneering work in brain surgery, which he carried on at his own private Institute in California.

"Would he come here?" she asked doubtfully. "I understand he only sees patients at his Institute."

"When Dexter opened it six years ago, I built him his pressurized operating theater."

"Built it?" Her eyes widened.

"Gave him the money to do so," the old man explained. "He will come to see Nico, my child, don't have any fears about that."

She half smiled. "Money has its uses after all."

"It would have more use if you spent some on yourself. Nico told me he's opened several accounts for you in Nice, but you refuse to use them."

"I wouldn't feel happy spending his money."

"He wants you to think of it as yours. It will distress him to learn you don't. You should be able to go out and buy anything your heart desires."

"It only desires Nicolas to be well," she said and burst into tears.

Appreciating this as a sign of the strain she was under, Mr. Panos did his best to comfort her, though she was still tearful as they entered the villa. Voices were coming from the salon, and almost at once Leon appeared.

He looked at Alex but spoke to his uncle, anxiously asking for the latest news of Nicolas. Alex listened quietly while the two men spoke and wondered why Mr. Panos had not told her his nephew had returned from Greece. Either he thought she did not care enough about him to be bothered or he was afraid she cared too much. With a start, she realized Leon was talking to her.

"Congratulations on your engagement, Alex. I was delighted when I heard about it."

"I was surprised when I heard of *yours*."

His eyes slid away from hers, turning with relief to look at his uncle, who was moving toward the stairs.

"I'm going to my room to rest," Mr. Panos said. "I will see you both later."

As he moved out of earshot, Leon spoke to her again. "I would never have left you and gone to Greece if you had agreed to marry me."

"Even though you were already engaged?"

"It was *only* an engagement. If you had loved me, I would have broken it."

"You could also have *told* me about it."

"You wouldn't have gone on seeing me if I had! I knew you didn't love me, and I wanted to make you change your mind. Then I would have told you the truth."

"That isn't true." Tired of subterfuge, she refused to let Leon continue with his pretence. "You loved me in your fashion—I won't deny it—but you also loved your position with your uncle. That's why you went to Greece. No one forced you to go."

"Is that what Nico told you?"

"Yes. And I believe him. Don't lie to me, Leon. With Nicolas so ill, at least have the courage to be honest."

He gave a heavy sigh. "Yes, I agreed to go to Greece," he said, "but only because I knew I wasn't the man to make you happy. Please forgive me, Alex."

"I'd find that easier to do if you hadn't let Nicolas think he might have to buy me off!"

"I never gave him that impression! I swear it. If Nico thought so, it was because he has always been suspicious of women. Believe me, Alex, I would never malign you to anyone."

She stared at him. It was pointless to continue this discussion, and, more to the point, it would become embarrassing. As Nicolas's wife, the Panos family would become hers, and that meant accepting Leon, too.

"Let's forget the past," she said quietly. "After all, meeting you led me to Nicolas."

His look was rueful, but he took her hands and raised them to his lips. "I won't do this in front of Nico. He can be murderously jealous."

Alex's own jealousy rose at these words, for they implied that Leon had seen Nicolas jealous before. Yet why shouldn't he have? Nicolas had never pretended he had lived the life of a monk. She remembered Elena and quickly pushed the girl from her mind.

"I think I'll follow Mr. Panos's example and go upstairs for a rest." She moved across the hall. "I'll see you at dinner, Leon."

Events moved swiftly in the next few days. Nicolas

did not improve, and his father arranged for Darrell Dexter to fly from America to see him.

Twenty-four hours later, the man arrived. He in no way resembled Sir Matthew, being small, dapper, and very jolly, but after a lengthy examination of his patient, he concurred with the Englishman's diagnosis.

"All I would suggest is that your son return home," he advised Mr. Panos and Alex. "He can start to do a little work, too. Enough to get his interest going. But he must still avoid stress." The neurosurgeon looked at his host. "And that means no arguments with *you,* my friend!"

"Nico and I do not argue," the old man growled. "We have disagreements, and we enjoy them!"

"Well, don't enjoy yourselves for the next few months! I want your son to lead an even-tempoed and even-tempered life!"

Mr. Panos chuckled and moved to the door. "I will come with you to the airport, Darrell. But first I will call the pilot and tell him we're on the way."

"A Panos jet to myself," the American murmured to Alex as they were left alone. "It is astonishing the amount of time it saved me." He gave her a searching look. "What is worrying you, Miss Godfrey? I promise you I've told the truth about your fiancé. In a few months, he should be completely fit and able to marry you."

Alex half turned away. "Does that—does that mean it wouldn't be advisable for us to marry now?"

"Not unless you keep it platonic. For the next few months, he must avoid all excitement!" He heard her sigh and gave her a keen look. "Is there anything else you want to ask me?"

She shook her head. What he had said made it perfectly clear she couldn't tell Nicolas about the night in the cottage. She did not know why this should suddenly distress her, since she had already decided never to tell him or at least not until they had been married long enough to feel secure with each other.

"We're ready to leave," Mr. Panos said, returning to the room. "Do you wish to come with us, Alex?"

Shaking her head, she retired to her room. A vague depression had settled over her, and she felt the need to be alone.

The following day, Nicolas returned to the villa, and for the first time Alex felt it to be a home and not merely a luxurious place in which to live. It was wonderful to come into a room and see him sitting there or to have him facing her across the table at mealtimes. But best of all were the afternoons, when Mr. Panos retired to his study, and she and Nicolas lounged by the pool and soaked up the sun until it disappeared below the horizon.

Then for the next hour, Nicolas would talk business with his father, and since this was conducted mainly in Greek, Alex went to her room to read and then bathe and change leisurely into one of her simple cotton dresses, coming down in time to join the men for predinner drinks.

After dinner, Mr. Panos usually went to visit his numerous friends along the coast. He enjoyed an active social life, and Alex became very conscious that this was the life that appealed to Nicolas too. She was not sure how much she would enjoy it herself and experienced her first qualms about the future. She was used to working for her living and could not envisage long days of doing nothing except shopping for clothes or gossiping with girlfriends. Besides, as the wife of the illustrious Nico Panos, which of her girlfriends would she still have?

But the recollection of Christoff Panos's first remark to her made her decide the future wouldn't be as boring as she feared. She and Nicolas might not have the five children he had suggested, but they would certainly have several, God willing. The thought of having a child of Nicolas's brought a tender look to her face, and, seeing it, Nicolas pulled her across the space between them to sit on his lap.

"You're so aloof these days," he complained. "Every time I kiss you, you act like an ice maiden."

"I've been given strict orders to keep you calm."

"Then you should wear a veil on your face and a blanket around your body!" He rubbed his cheek upon hers. "I'm well again, Alex, but I'll have a relapse if you keep me so frustrated."

"I'm sorry," she apologized, "but I can't do anything about it."

"Well, I can!" He proceeded to do so in a way that set the blood pounding through her body and awoke memories of the last time he had held her so passionately.

"It's crazy for us to waste time like this," he muttered. "Marry me now, Alex. As soon as I can get the license."

"Are you sure?"

"Of course I'm sure! Neither of us will have any peace of mind until you're my wife." He gave a deep sigh. "And I certainly won't have any peace of body!

So, do I have your permission to set the day?" At her silent nod, he hugged her close. "Six days from now, my dearest, and we'll tie the knot. Providing I can pull enough strings with the authorities."

"Six days," she echoed. "I can't believe it."

"'You'll believe it on the morning of the seventh day," he whispered and tickled her ear with his tongue. "You'd better lock your door tonight, my angel. I'm a wild Greek, and I find you too tempting!"

Happy at the thought of her impending marriage, Alex went to bed. Tonight she was more reassured about Nicolas's improvement than at any time since his accident. It was hard to believe it was seven weeks since it had happened, and she was guiltily aware that for the past three weeks Eleanor had been running the café on her own. But, luckily, a few days before, a Danish girl had offered to help out for the summer, and she was proving capable and willing.

Alex had told Nicolas about it, and with characteristic generosity, he had suggested they install Eleanor in a villa along the coast and provide her with sufficient income to maintain it. Alex had been overwhelmed by the offer, and her reaction had astonished him, for he regarded the woman as a part of his wife's family and, as such, a part of his commitment to maintain. It was an aspect of Greek tradition that Alex found particularly heartwarming, and she mused on it as she settled down to sleep.

It was only as she relaxed that she became aware of a nagging pain in her intestines. She had been feeling unwell for a couple of days and had toyed with the idea of going to see Dr. Hugo. Now she began to regret not having gone today, for the ache was slowly getting worse. She breathed deeply and slowly, and after a while the pain eased sufficiently for her to fall into an uneasy slumber.

It was still dark when she awoke and the house had that special quality of stillness that told her all its occupants were asleep. The ache in her lower stomach had become a persistent pain, and she stumbled into the bathroom and rummaged in the cupboard for some aspirins. As she did so, she felt as if a steel band was gripping her round her waist, and she sank gasping to the floor. This was no ordinary stomach upset, she knew, and she wondered if it were appendicitis. Whatever it was, it could not be ignored, and though reluctant to arouse the household, she was too frightened to wait until morning.

Pressing her hands to her stomach, she staggered along the corridor to Nicolas's room. Quietly she opened the door and went in. He was fast asleep and did not stir at her entry, and she moved over to the bed and touched his shoulder.

"Nicolas," she whispered. "Nicolas, wake up."

"Alex?" he said thickly and then sat bolt upright. "What's wrong?"

"I have an awful pain. I think you'd better call the doctor."

She was still talking as he switched on his bedside lamp, and, seeing her ashen face, he jumped out of bed and caught her up in his arms. He carried her back to her room as effortlessly as if she were a child and placed her on the bed. Then he dialed the extension to his valet and barked something to him in

Greek before he bent over Alex again and stared at her with worried eyes.

"How long have you been like this? Do you think it's something you ate?"

"I don't know. I've been feeling queasy for several days."

"Why didn't you tell me?"

"I didn't want to worry you."

"You worry me more by keeping it a secret. You are never to hide anything from me. Do you hear that Alex? Never!"

She adored his solicitude and, since the pain had momentarily eased, was able to give him a wan smile. But then another cramp seized her, and she had to bite her lip hard to stop herself from crying out.

"Hang on, darling," Nicolas whispered. "Dr. Margrave should be here soon."

He continued to murmur words of comfort to her, and he was sitting by her side when the doctor bustled into the room. With a reassuring smile, he went out, and, as the door closed behind him, another spasm gripped Alex, more violent than any she had yet experienced. She cried aloud, and the doctor pulled aside the bedclothes and bent to examine her.

For the next half hour, she had no clear recollection of what was happening to her beyond the fact that the cramps became worse and she was bleeding. Then, miraculously, all pain ceased, leaving her as exhausted as if she had run a mile.

"It's over, my dear," Dr. Margrave said. "You may have a little more discomfort, but I do not think it necessary to send you to the Clinic."

Only then did the full knowledge of what had happened dawn on her, and she gave a little cry and buried her head in the pillow. How could she have been so naïve not to have guessed?

"I had no symptoms of being pregnant," she whispered.

"There is usually one unfailing sign," the doctor said.

"I know," Alex murmured, "but I—I thought that the stress of Nicolas being ill had upset me. I never realized. . . . "

"Well, it's over now," the doctor repeated. "All you need is a few days in bed and then a checkup with a specialist in a few weeks' time. Meanwhile, I will give you an injection to help you relax and then arrange for a nurse to come and look after you."

"I don't need an injection," she protested.

Without replying, he deftly slipped a needle into her vein. "This way is much better for you," he said soothingly. "It's been a shock for you, and a long sleep will make you feel better."

"I don't need a nurse," she said weakly.

"I'm sure Mr. Panos would want you to have one."

"He doesn't. . . . " Alex struggled to speak. Her head was beginning to swim, and her mouth felt dry. She knew she had something important to say, but she could not control her thoughts. It was something to do with Nicolas. He mustn't be told the truth. Darrell Dexter had warned her he mustn't have any shocks or excitement, and if he learned what had happened to her, he would be furious with himself.

"Don't tell. . . . " she mumbled. "Nicolas mustn't. . . ."

"Relax and sleep," the doctor soothed her. "There's nothing to worry about."

She tried to say more, but her tongue was too heavy to move. With an incoherent murmur, she pointed to the door and then lost consciousness.

Chapter Eleven

Alex awoke to the presence of a white starched apron and a pink-and-white-striped dress. A nurse of any nationality was a reassuring sight and particularly this one, who, to Alex's surprise, was English.

"You have had an excellent sleep," she said as she saw Alex's eyes upon her. "Do you feel better?"

"Yes, thank you. What time is it?"

"Two o'clock."

"You mean I've slept the whole night and a morning?"

"And part of the afternoon, too."

Alex looked down at herself and saw she was wearing a fresh nightdress.

"I washed you and changed you, and you didn't bat an eyelash," the nurse added.

"I must have had a strong sedative. No wonder my head feels woozy."

"You'll feel steadier once you've had something to eat. Do you think you can manage some tea and toast?"

"Yes, please. With some jam, too. I'm starving."

The nurse went out, and Alex dozed again. When she awoke for the second time, it was to see a beautifully laid tray on a trolley in front of her.

"Doesn't it make your mouth water?"

The nurse pointed to a pile of buttery toast, and Alex struggled up into a sitting position. The room swam alarmingly, and she closed her eyes.

"Have some tea first," the nurse suggested and proceeded to pour a cup.

By the time Alex had drunk it, she was feeling considerably steadier, and after her second cup, she felt so much better that she debated whether to get dressed.

"You'd be wiser to stay in bed for a couple of days," the nurse advised. "I know you were barely pregnant, but it's always best to take things easy after something like this."

Barely pregnant. The words almost made Alex smile. How many girls must have shuddered when they heard a similar expression, yet how happy she would have been had she been aware of it at the time. Or would she? She pondered the question and then concluded that what had happened was for the best. The first year of her marriage to Nicolas would bring enough difficult adjustments for them both without their having to cope with a child.

She sighed and leaned back on the pillows. There were still so many facets of his character that were alien to her, as there were many aspects of her own nature that were alien to him, and it would take time before these differences were understood and appreciated. To bring a child into their life before this happened would only lead to an extra burden. Besides which, a child should be born of true love, not be the result of delirium. How distressed Nicolas would be when he learned the truth.

With a cry, she sat up and the nurse looked at her anxiously.

"Is anything wrong, Miss Godfrey?"

"Do you know if Dr. Margrave has told Mr. Panos about me? Mr. Nicolas Panos?"

"They were talking together downstairs when I arrived here last night."

"How did he seem? Was he upset?"

The freckles on the nurse's cheeks faded as her color rose to match them. "He was most distressed. I think it was a great shock to him."

"It was a shock to me, too," Alex whispered. "I never even knew."

For an instant, the nurse looked startled, then she came swiftly to the side of the bed. "What an unpleasant shock for you."

"It must have been worse for Nicolas," Alex whispered and then set her lips tight, knowing she dare not say more. But the thought of his state of mind when he had learned the truth from the doctor filled her with anguish.

"Do you think I could see my fiancé?" she asked.

"Of course. I'll see if I can find him for you. But don't get out of bed while I'm away."

As Alex waited for Nicolas, she rehearsed what she

would say to him and wondered how she could make him see he must not blame himself for what had occurred. She remembered those agonizing moments when she had fought against his frenzied need of her, when she had vainly sought to evade his kisses and his touch. What irony that such a union had almost resulted in a child!

A tap on the door brought her into an upright position, and color flooded her face as Nicolas came in. He was as pale as he had been on the night of his accident, when he had lain unconscious on the ground. But this time his eyes were not closed; they were open and looking at her with a blankness she had not seen since that night, either. A tremor of fear uncurled within her.

"D-don't look so worried, Nicolas. I'm feeling much better. P-perfectly well, in fact. I'm sure I'll be able to get up tomorrow."

"Good. I will make arrangements for you to leave."

"Leave where?"

"Here." The word was clipped. "Or do you think I'm so besotted over you that I will let you remain in my home now I know the truth?"

Not sure if her ears were playing her false, she stared at him blankly.

Seeing her expression, his eyes sparked with fury and seemed to ignite the emotion he had been holding in check.

"What do you take me for?" he grated. "It was hard enough to forget you'd been Leon's girlfriend! How did you expect me to react when I found you'd been his mistress as well!" His voice thickened. "How dare you agree to marry me when you were expecting another man's child! Don't you have any sense of shame?"

Still she went on staring at him, trying to make sense of what he was saying. But only one thing was clear. Nicolas had no recollection of what had happened at the cottage. He believed Leon was responsible. She put her hands to her head. Even worse, he believed her guilty of a deception so appalling that she could not bear to think of it. Yet think of it she must, for she had to make him see how wrong he was.

"You don't understand," she whispered shakily. "It wasn't—it isn't the way you think."

"I *didn't* think where you were concerned," he said savagely. "My love for you blinded me. But I can see you clearly now, and—"

"You can't!" she cried. "You don't know the truth. Do you think I agreed to marry you knowing I was expecting another man's child?"

"Yes."

"You're wrong. It wasn't like that at all."

She moistened her lips. She had to tell him the truth, yet she was unsure where to begin, how to find the right words, how to minimize the shock it was going to be for him. And after the shock would come his remorse, which would be even harder for him to bear.

"Why didn't you tell me the truth?" he demanded. "Were you afraid that if I found out I would stop loving you?" He flung up his hands. "Perhaps I would. I don't know. All I can think of is that you lied to me. That you were prepared to marry me carrying another man's child!"

He turned away as if he could not bear the sight of her, and she looked at his back, tall and straight, and the tilt of his head with its thick, glossy black hair. She knew she should feel anger, yet all she felt was compassion. Poor, misguided Nicolas.

"You don't understand." Her voice was so thin that she had to clear her throat. "You're wrong, Nicolas. It wasn't Leon who. . . . He was never my lover. It was *you*."

"Me?" With a lightning movement, he swung round on her. "Did you say *me*?"

"Yes." Her eyes filled with tears. "Oh darling, don't you remember?"

His eyes widened and then narrowed into dark, glittering slits. His mouth set into a straight hard line, and his jaw clenched so tightly that the muscles bunched along the sides of his neck. "Did you say *me*?" he repeated slowly.

"Yes. It was at the cottage. The night you had a fever. You were delirious, and I went into your room to see if I could calm you."

"And that's when I seduced you?"

"Yes." Her voice shook. "Don't you remember *anything*?"

"There's nothing to remember," he snapped. "You must think me a fool if you expect me to believe a story like that."

"It isn't a story. It's the truth."

She could not believe he was denying what she had said. Never in her wildest dreams had she thought this would happen.

"It's the truth, Nicolas. I swear it. You were delirious and you made love to me. I tried to fight you, but I . . . you were too strong and I couldn't stop you from. . . ." She started to cry. "You've got to believe me. I swear it, Nicolas. By everything I hold dear, I swear it."

She leaned towards him, arms outstretched, her agitation so deep that she was unaware of pushing the bedclothes aside, uncaring that her slender body was clearly visible beneath the diaphanous folds of her nightdress. All she knew was that Nicolas thought she was lying.

"I was never Leon's girlfriend. I went out with him because he was fun. But it's you I love."

"Spare me any more of your lies! I may have suffered a blow on the head, but it didn't knock out my brains!"

"It's made you forget the truth."

"The truth?" He leaned menacingly towards her. "Be careful what you say to me, Alex, or I may try and strangle the truth out of you!" His hands moved upwards as if itching to put themselves around her throat.

Aghast, she recoiled from him, unable to believe this wasn't some nightmare from which she would awaken. She couldn't be pleading like this with Nicolas. He couldn't be refusing to believe what she had said.

But he was. She could see it in the dark eyes that were regarding her with contempt.

Drawing a shuddering breath, she gathered her courage around her. "You did make love to me that night at the cottage. I tried to fight you, but you were too strong and . . . and I couldn't."

"Why didn't you tell me about it the next day?" he demanded.

"Because Dr. Hugo said you weren't to have any excitement."

"You mean *he* knows the truth."

"No—no he doesn't." Alex saw the light die in Nicolas's eyes. "I was too embarrassed to tell him. Anyway, there was no point in his knowing."

"Because there was *nothing* for him to know! I give you full marks for persistence, Alex, but you aren't succeeding! You were already pregnant when you agreed to marry me." Nicolas enunciated each word with dreadful precision. "You were going to wait until we had been married a month, and you would then have come to me with your wonderful news. That's the real truth, isn't it? You were going to foist Leon's love child onto me!"

"How can you think such a thing? On your own admission, there are several hours of that night that are a blank to you. Why can't you believe me when I tell you what happened?"

"Because I'd never forget a thing like that! I'm not crazy," he said savagely. "Do you think I'd ravish the woman I love and then forget it?"

"You *have* forgotten!" She almost screamed the words. "Believe me, Nicolas. For God's sake, believe me!"

"Never! It's over, Alex. You can't turn my head any more." His voice was hard as stone. "Dry those lovely eyes of yours and pull the covers 'round your beautiful body, which I'm supposed to have deflowered one unremembered night! The game's over, and so is our future." He went to the door and, from a distance of several yards, regarded her. "It was an excellent try, and it nearly came off. If it had occurred a month from now, you would have succeeded in fooling me.

As it is . . . . " His mouth turned down at the corner. "Good-bye, Alex. I hope we never meet again."

The door closed quietly behind him; the very softness of the sound made his departure more final, showing her his words had not been said in the heat of temper but in cold blood.

Pushing her hair away from her tear-streaked face, Alex staggered out of bed. It was impossible for her to stay here. Weak or not, she must leave at once.

"What on earth do you think you're doing?" Coming back into the room, the nurse regarded her with astonishment.

"I'm leaving." Alex turned from the dressing table where she was making an effort to hide her blotchy skin with powder. "Please don't waste time arguing with me, nurse. I'm sorry you were called in unnecessarily, but—"

"Forget that," the nurse interrupted. "All I'm concerned with is you. You're not in a fit state to go anywhere."

"I must." Alex looked vaguely 'round the room. "If you could help me to pack and then call a taxi . . . . "

"Just sit quietly and leave it to me," the nurse replied. "If you've definitely made up your mind to go, I'd rather you walked out than were carried out!"

Alex did not see Nicolas or any of the family when she left the villa an hour later. Going shakily down the stairs, with no one to greet her or to say good-bye, she felt like a servant who had been wrongfully dismissed. One day Nicolas would recover his memory and, when he did, she hoped the anguish he experienced would be as bitter as the anguish he had inflicted upon *her*. Perhaps by the time his memory returned, he would be married to another woman, even be the father of her children. The thought of this was more than she could bear, and she clutched at the banisters and fought for her control.

"Would you like me to come to the taxi with you?" the nurse asked. "I don't think you should be alone."

"I'll be fine once I'm away from here." With an effort, Alex continued down the stairs.

"What shall I say to the doctor?" Once more the nurse spoke. "He'll have my hide for letting you go like this."

"Tell him you couldn't stop me."

Alex quickened her pace, afraid that the nurse might forcibly restrain her from leaving. Through the half-open front door she glimpsed the taxi and almost ran the last few steps to it.

Only as she climbed into the back seat did she relax. "Don't worry about me, nurse. I'll be fine once I'm in my own home."

"I thought *this* was your home."

"No. It never was. It was just a dream."

Unable to continue speaking, Alex signaled the driver to move.

"Good-bye, Miss Godfrey," the nurse called. "Take care of yourself."

"Take care." Alex swallowed a sob. How did one take care of a broken heart? Of shattered hopes? Of a life that had lost its meaning? Tears blinded her, and she blinked her lids. I mustn't cry, she told herself. I must forget everything . . . the way Nicolas has forgotten.

Because there was no telephone at the cottage, it had not been possible to warn Eleanor of her return, and as the taxi went slowly down the uneven lane, she rummaged in her bag for the key, breathing a sigh of relief when she found she still had it.

But there was no need to use it, for at the taxi's approach, Eleanor came onto the terrace to see who it was, her face expressing surprise and then concern as she saw her goddaughter.

At the sight of Eleanor, Alex's intentions of remaining calm came to nothing, and, dropping her case to the ground, she flung herself into her godmother's arms and burst into another flood of tears.

Later, curled up in the settee, the whole unhappy story told, she felt considerably calmer, though the same could not be said of Eleanor, who was furious.

"You were crazy to have left the way you did. You should have insisted on seeing Nicolas again and making him listen to you. I'm sure he would have believed you eventually."

"He wouldn't. If you had seen his face . . . the way he looked at me." Alex shivered at the memory. "He never loved me. If he did, he wouldn't have thought me capable of such deceit."

"Jealousy can turn a man into a fool," Eleanor said crisply. "When he's cooled down, he'll come to his senses."

"He won't," Alex sighed. "It's over." She looked at her fingers, bare as they had always been. Her engagement had been so short there had not been time for Nicolas to buy her a ring.

"I'm sure he still loves you," the older woman reaffirmed. "If he didn't, he wouldn't have been so insane with anger."

"He desired me," Alex contradicted. "That's different from love."

"What are you going to do now?" Eleanor asked bluntly. "If you're really convinced you and Nicolas are through, I don't think you should stay on here."

"I won't. I'll wire Sherry tomorrow and fly home at the end of the week."

"Good." Eleanor stood up. "But right now, the only place you're going is bed. We'll talk again tomorrow."

To her surprise, Alex slept well, though more from exhaustion than peace of mind, and awoke with the dull ache of having lost Nicolas forever. Eleanor was right: the sooner she returned to London and concentrated on her career, the better; and if she could not find stage work, she would look around for something else.

After breakfast, she went to the village to send a telegram to Sherry. The climb up the hill tired her, and she made a leisurely pace on her way back. It was only as she turned into the lane and saw the huge car parked at the bottom of it that her heart began to beat like a wild thing. Had Nicolas accepted her story after all? She began to run and, only as she reached the terrace steps and saw Christoff Panos sitting on the balustrade, did her excitement vanish, leaving her so bereft that it was all she could do to summon the strength to walk up the steps to greet him.

"I have come for an explanation," he said without preamble. "What is wrong between you and Nico? Why did you run away from the house without seeing me?"

Discomfited, she stared at him. If Nicolas had not told his father the truth, she could not do so either.

"Well?" he said impatiently. "Tell me."

"I would rather you asked your son."

"Do you think I haven't? But he refuses to tell me. He says I should mind my own business. Me, his father!"

He flung his hands heavenwards, and Alex could not help a slight smile. What a warmhearted man he was, and how she would love to have been his daughter-in-law. Quickly she shied away from the thought.

"Will you tell me why you and Nicolas quarreled?" he asked again. "Or must I remain in ignorance for the rest of my life?"

Alex moistened her lips. Instinctively, she knew that Christoff Panos would believe her story. But what would happen then? He would rush back to the coast and confront his son. He might well get Leon to swear he had never made love to her. Perhaps he could even achieve the final miracle and convince Nicolas that it was true.

The thought of this was so sweet that she longed to believe it. Yet even as she tried, the sweetness was engulfed by bitterness. Nicolas had to believe in her honesty because it was something he felt deep down inside himself. If his doubts were only dissolved because *other* people had faith in her, then she would always be afraid he would doubt her again. And a lasting marriage could never be built on such a shaky foundation.

Slowly she raised her head and looked at Mr. Panos. "We stopped loving each other," she lied. "Luckily we realized it in time."

"Why did Dr. Margrave come to the house?"

"I had a bilious attack."

"A lot of things seem to have happened to you in the course of one day," the old man said bluntly. "I do not believe you are telling me the truth."

"I'm sorry," she said politely and half turned towards the cottage. "Would you like some coffee?"

"Your godmother is making me a cup."

As if on cue, Eleanor came across the terrace with a tray.

Mr. Panos drank thirstily and accepted a second cup. He ignored Alex and concentrated on charming Eleanor, making Alex realize from where Nicolas had inherited his ability to turn a woman's head.

It was an hour before he made his departure, and she walked with him to the car.

"You still love Nico," he said. "I can see it in your eyes."

There was no answer she could give, and she remained silent.

"And my son loves *you*," he continued. "If he didn't, he would be pleased that you had gone. Instead of which he behaves like a bear with a bellyache."

"No one likes to admit they've made a mistake," she said carefully. "In a few weeks' time, he will have forgotten me."

"And will you have forgotten him?"

"I have my work," she said flatly.

"My son is a fool!" Christoff Panos exclaimed. "And you are a fool, too. But if neither of you will tell me the truth, then I cannot help you."

"Sometimes people have to be left alone to work out their own destinies."

"In other words, you are also telling me to mind my own business?"

"Don't be angry with me," she pleaded.

"I am only angry that you will not be my daughter-in-law." He put his lips to her brow and then climbed into the car.

"Good-bye, Mr. Panos," she said as calmly as she could.

"*Au revoir,*" he replied through the open window. "I refuse to believe this is the end."

She turned away, unwilling for him to see her tears. Despite his conviction that they would meet again, she herself held no such belief; to think otherwise would only make it more difficult to forget Nicolas. And she must forget him. It was her only salvation.

Chapter Twelve

Anticipating fruitless days spent making the theatrical rounds, Alex was delighted to receive a call from her agent the morning after she returned to London, asking her to read for the female lead in a new West End play.

Warning herself not to be optimistic, she went to the theater on Monday of the following week and, as she had expected, found seven other girls auditioning for the same role.

She forced herself not to think of the competition in case it made her nervous and was surprised by the calmness with which she approached the reading. Yet when she analyzed her reaction, the reason was easy to appreciate. Having loved and lost Nicolas, there was nothing else that could affect her deeply. To lose a role in a West End play—no matter how important it was—meant nothing when compared with the fact that she had lost the only man she would ever love.

Even when her audition was over and she was asked to stay behind, she did so without any sense of excitement, despite knowing that the role of Liza Court, a women's liberationist of the nineteen eighties, was a magnificent part guaranteed to make the name of any actress lucky enough to play it.

Steps stopped in front of her, and she looked up and saw a grey-haired man of medium height.

"I'm Jack Geddie. Producer and director of the show," he smiled. "I've come to offer my congratulations."

"You mean I've got the part?"

He nodded. "We start rehearsals Tuesday week. Four weeks later, we go on tour for a month and then bring the play into town."

Joyously, Alex returned home to tell Sherry her news and also to write to Eleanor. It was exactly the sort of thing that would reassure her godmother that she was rebuilding her life. Today a kindly fate had sent her on the first step; the rest was up to her.

The next month was one of the most difficult Alex had ever spent. Not for nothing did Jack Geddie have the reputation of being the toughest man in show business. He insisted on the maximum effort from everyone the whole time. He expected all the cast to be word perfect in their parts on the first day of rehearsal and ready to stay on stage long after normal working hours were over. But because he was considered to be the golden man of the theater—who had never produced a failure—no one objected to the pressure or refused to comply with his orders.

Sometimes Alex was so exhausted that she felt like handing in her resignation, but as soon as she returned home and was more rested, she knew she would not trade the part of Liza Court for anything in the world.

Yet she could not forget Nicolas. The thought of him set her heart pounding, and the sight of a dark-haired man in the street made her weak at the knees. Whenever the telephone rang or there was a knock at the door, her pulses betrayed her, and she wondered despairingly how long she would go on hoping he would come to his senses. It was six weeks since she had left France, and there had been no word from him. It was unrealistic to think he would call her now.

"What are you doing this evening?" Jack Geddie's voice made her turn 'round from the stage door, where she had paused to collect some makeup that had been left for her.

"Nothing," she murmured. "Don't tell me you want me for another rehearsal?"

"I want you for myself," he smiled. "You are going to have dinner with me. Any objections?"

"None," she said calmly and went on her way.

Jack Geddie's invitation was unwelcome but not unexpected, for he was reputed to have had affairs with all his young leading ladies. But it would have been unwise to have refused his invitation, though she would probably have to be unwise in the end. Still, she would do her best to make him see she was not interested in anything beyond a mild flirtation.

Two weeks later and after five more dinners with him, he had still not justified her fears and, opposite him in a Soho restaurant to which he had taken her after an unusually long rehearsal, she had to concede that his company had helped her to put Nicolas into perspective. She had not stopped loving him—that was something that would take her years to do—but at least she no longer cried herself to sleep at night and was able to get through each day without continually thinking of him.

"Done your packing yet?" Jack asked, for they were leaving on their provincial tour at the weekend.

"I'm not taking much," she replied. "Knowing you, we won't have time for socializing. I bet you'll make stage changes after every performance!"

"That's what an out-of-town tryout is for. But *you* will be expected to socialize daily—with me."

"Is that the boss's orders?"

"No," he said sharply. "You are free to refuse me, if that's what you wish."

"Really?" She half smiled. "You wouldn't like it if I did."

"Of course I wouldn't. But don't see my invitations to you as a threat."

"Thank you for saying that, Jack."

"I've been wanting to say it for quite a while." He hesitated, then deliberately steered the conversation towards her personal life, which he had also done the last time he had taken her out.

"Why are you so curious about my past?" she asked.

"It's the best way of discovering if I can become part of your future!"

"You already are. This play is in for a long run."

"I'm talking about your private life, Alex, not your professional one."

"I have no private life, Jack. My career means everything to me."

"That isn't true. You aren't hard-boiled enough. You're a vulnerable girl, and you've been badly hurt in the past. It sticks out a mile." He frowned. "But the past should be forgotten. It's the future you must consider. How about being my girl, Alex?"

"I don't want to be anyone's girl."

"I won't take no for an answer," he warned. "I'm falling in love with you."

"Please don't," she said quickly. "I'm not ready for anything serious."

"But you aren't interested in playing around either, are you?"

"No!"

It was a harsh sound, and Jack smiled. "You can't live your life in limbo, my angel."

"It isn't limbo to live without a man!"

"It's a waste of a beautiful piece of merchandise!" He touched the golden hair that reached to her shoulders. "You aren't only a genuine blonde, Alex, you're a genuine girl. I *am* in love with you, you know, and you *will* get over him."

Startled, she avoided his eyes, not sure if he had heard any rumors of her brief association with Nicolas or if it was merely a shot in the dark.

"It's obvious," Jack continued, answering her unspoken question. "When a lovely girl says she isn't interested in a man, it can only be because of another man."

Silently she gathered up her handbag, and, taking the hint, Jack called for the bill.

True to expectations, the provincial tour necessitated many alterations to the play, but on their opening night in London, they received a standing ovation and knew they had a hit on their hands.

Spirits ran high, metaphorically and literally, at the first-night party, which took place in a private room at the Savoy, where everyone congratulated each other and Jack Geddie's arrival received a burst of applause.

Standing in a corner sipping champagne, Alex watched him talking to the group of men who had backed the show and knew that as soon as he could, he would come and join her. During the provincial tour he had not reopened the subject of having an affair with her, though his demands for her company had increased, and she foresaw that in the not-too-distant future she would have to face and solve the problem he posed. Yet for the moment, she was determined to live each day as it came.

"Penny for your thoughts." He was standing in front of her and touched the edge of her champagne glass with his own.

"I was thinking how pleased you must be about the play," she said at once.

"I start work on a new one next week."

"Don't you ever take a holiday?"

"Never alone. Care to come with me? Okay, I know the answer to that one!" He stopped a passing waiter and took two more glasses of champagne, one of which he gave to Alex. "Having firmly put me in my place as a Dutch uncle," he continued, "I hope you're free to come with me to a party on Saturday night."

"It will have to be after the theater," she said gravely. "My producer is a difficult man and would be furious if I missed a performance."

"He would strangle you by your lovely neck!" Jack chuckled.

"Whose party is it?" Alex asked.

"Dick Liandris. It's a coming-out party for his daughter, Tina. It'll be a lavish affair. You know what Greeks are."

Alex clasped her hands closely 'round her glass to stop them from shaking. "I'm afraid I don't," she said stiffly. "Greek tycoons are not in my orbit."

"I'm sure plenty of them would like to be. They go for blondes. I suppose it's because they're so dark themselves."

The conversation was becoming unbearable, and she wished there were a way of ending it. "Do you know Mr. Liandris well?"

"We were at Oxford together—which should tell you how old I am!" He grinned at her. "Tina's a pretty child. Not so much of a child actually. The party is to announce her engagement. Which reminds me . . ." he lowered his voice, "have *you* had a change of heart recently?"

"Only a hardening."

"You're a cruel young woman," he sighed, "but I still love you." He caught her hand and, careless who might be watching, raised it to his lips. "In case I forgot to tell you, your performance tonight was magnificent."

"Honestly?"

"I'm not flattering you. I don't need a conquest that badly!"

The truth of his compliment was fortified by the critics the following day, for all of them sighted her performance as the best thing the stage had seen for years. Her agent was inundated with other offers for her, but she was under firm contract to Jack Geddie and knew he would never release her until the play closed—which might not be for several years. It was exhilarating to know she need not worry about finding work for a long time to come, though she was afraid of becoming stale in her part if she continued to play it for too long.

"You've been offered the lead in Boris Smith's new film," her agent informed her on the telephone a couple of days after the play had opened in London. "He saw your performance last night, and he's just called me. It's a great opportunity, honey, and he's offering a fortune."

"You know I can't take it," she protested. "I have to be at the theater each night at seven, and there's a Wednesday matinee too."

"Boris says you can be back in town by six and no shooting on Wednesday."

"He must want me pretty badly."

"He does," her agent said happily. "Everyone's talking about your Liza. Even *I* am impressed by you! That speech of yours where you say you'll never allow yourself to fall in love makes my blood run cold every time I hear it. You say it as if you mean it."

"I do," she said smoothly. "Aren't you pleased I'm so career-minded!"

He chuckled. "I'm just grateful to the bastard who's made you a man-hater!"

She laughed, but her humor was only surface-deep. How surprised Max would be if he knew she meant every word of Liza's speech, that she was not just saying it to the man in the play but to Nicolas, who had loved her without understanding her, who had been so quick to condemn her. Nicolas. The name was still a torment as was the thought of him.

"Will you go and see Boris?" her agent asked.

"I'll talk to Jack first."

"Since when is *he* your agent?"

"He's my friend," she said swiftly.

"Then let him take care of your private life, and leave me to take care of your public one!"

She was smiling as she replaced the receiver, and she firmly kept her thoughts focused on the bright success ahead of her. Her future was assured, and her bank balance was increasing appreciably each week. If she accepted Boris Smith's offer, it would increase even more.

The knowledge persuaded her to buy a new dress for the Liandris party. According to Jack, all the world and his wife would be there, and it was good for her career to be seen in the social swing. Actresses needed publicity to keep their names before the public, and attending glamorous parties was all part of the new life she was making for herself.

Determinedly, she thought of Saturday and all the other Saturdays to come, but as always the truth outweighed the glamor, and she sank onto a chair and stared sightlessly in front of her, knowing she would give up her career for one single hour in Nicolas's arms.

Chapter Thirteen

When the night of the Liandris party arrived, Alex regretted her promise to go to it with Jack. A week of performances had left her physically depleted, and she wanted nothing more than to go straight home to bed.

But surveying herself in her dressing-room mirror after she had changed into the dress she had bought for the occasion, her regret vanished. There was nothing more likely to boost a woman's ego and chase away her fatigue than to know she looked her loveliest.

With more money to spend than usual, she had gone to a famous designer-dressmaker, and the result was a creation of ethereal demureness. Tiered and full-skirted, her dress was a cascade of palest pink silk, gossamer silver lace, and knife-pleated chiffon the same gold as her hair. The neckline was low, and the sleeves fell in a tier of lacy frills that matched the skirt. With her hair caught away from her face and falling in ringlets over one shoulder, she could have posed for a Romney portrait.

"You look sensational," was Jack's greeting as he came into her dressing room.

"Flatterer!"

"It's an understatement," he protested. "No hyperbole could begin to do you justice."

Driving through the dark streets towards Belgravia, she felt like Cinderella going to the ball, except that Jack's Mercedes would never turn into a pumpkin, and, come midnight, her only problem would be to keep awake! As they neared the Liandris house a long line of cars made them decide to park where they were and walk the remaining distance.

"I didn't know it was going to be such a big party," she commented.

"Six hundred guests and an orchestra flown in from New York."

"What a waste of money."

"If you have it," Jack said, "why not spend it? Liandris inherited it honestly."

"He didn't work for it?"

"I've yet to meet a Greek who doesn't work! No matter how many millions they have, they're never idle. And Dick's no exception."

"Do you see him often?"

"Every few months. He backs most of my plays. He's got money in yours, by the way."

She smiled. "Now I know why you wanted to show me off!"

He squeezed her arm. "You'd better watch out. Dick has an eye for a pretty girl and likes to keep his address book filled!"

Alex's sniff was expressive, and Jack chuckled. "You can always put him off by telling him you're *my* girl-friend."

"I can put him off by saying no," she said tartly. "It's a word women should use more often."

"Don't be too hard on Dick. His marriage was arranged when he was eighteen, and he's always looked for his amusement elsewhere. I only hope it won't be the same with Tina; she's a sweet kid."

"Do you know her fiancé?"

"Only by repute. He's Greek, of course, and rolling in money. A nephew of Christoff Panos's."

Alex stumbled and nearly fell.

"Caught your heel?" Jack asked.

"Y-yes." She bent down to her shoe, anxious to keep Jack's eyes off her face until she had managed to control herself. What an idiot she was not to have asked the name of Tina Liandris's fiancé. And it had been equally idiotic not to remember that Greek married Greek and, in the small and select world of such enormous wealth, there were only a few families able to supply acceptable suitors.

She debated whether to plead illness and not go to the party, then dismissed the idea as impractical. Jack was too astute not to see it as an excuse and wouldn't rest until he had discovered the real reason. She had no alternative but to face the evening with as much courage as she could muster.

Obviously Nicolas would be here. Never had she

thought to see him again. His world was so different from hers that she had believed she would live the rest of her life without seeing him.

But no, she was not being honest with herself; she had hoped they would meet again one day. She wanted him to come in search of her; she wanted him to writhe with shame and grovel at her feet. But above all she wanted to throw his love back in his face and tell him that love without faith was valueless.

"Fixed the shoe?" Jack asked, and with a nod, she straightened and walked with him to the house.

The party was held in an enormous marquee erected in the garden. It was astonishing to realize the great tent was made of canvas, so realistic did it look, with satin-draped walls and gilt chandeliers shining down on small, damask-covered tables. Couples were dancing on a raised floor, and clusters of people were wandering from table to table, greeting and being greeted.

The women bore out Alex's expectation, being lavishly gowned and jeweled, with many pretty ones squired by elderly men. Deliberately, she refused to scan the crowd for sight of any of the Panos family, knowing that sooner or later she would at least have to meet Leon. If only she could be sure of keeping out of Nicolas's way.

Her encounter with Leon came sooner than she had expected. She was chatting with her host and hostess when she felt a hand on her arm and heard his voice, high with astonishment, as he greeted her.

"Alex! What a wonderful surprise. I never expected to see you here."

Slowly she turned and looked at him. He was standing with his fiancée, a pretty, dark-haired girl, and she congratulated them both and then backed towards Jack, who was still talking to Dick Liandris.

"Oh no you don't," Leon said quietly, retaining his grip on her arm. "Now I've found you, I intend talking to you."

It was foolish to pretend not to know what he meant, and she allowed him to lead her away from the group.

"What happened between you and Nico?" he demanded as soon as they were out of earshot. "And don't fob off an excuse on me. I want the truth."

"We decided we didn't love each other."

"*Who* decided?"

"Both of us. Our engagement was a mistake."

"It may have been a mistake for you," he said gravely, "but it wasn't for Nico. He's been impossible since you parted."

With an effort she forced herself to smile. "If I remember correctly, you were always complaining that you found him impossible!"

"Then let's say he's even more impossible! He works and plays like a demon and doesn't relax for a second. Worse still, he won't let anyone else relax, either."

"Is he here?" she asked casually.

"Naturally. So is my uncle. You're bound to see them."

"I don't see why. There are hundreds of people here."

"But you stand out above all of them, my beautiful Alex," he said softly. "But then you always did." With a deep sigh, he moved back a couple of steps and slipped his arm around his fiancée's waist. "I hope you will come to our wedding, Alex. We're getting married in a month's time."

Nodding politely but silently vowing that nothing on earth would induce her to go, Alex rejoined Jack, who was still in conversation with his host.

He turned to her at once, drawing her close to his side. "Forgive me for talking business, darling, but I'm telling Dick about the large profits you and I are making for him!"

"I was at the first night," Dick Liandris told her. "I thought you gave an astonishing performance." He glanced over his shoulder and, seeing his wife talking to someone else, murmured: "I hope you'll be free to have lunch with me one day next week?"

"The week after would be better," Alex lied. "May I ring you and confirm what day I can make it?"

"If you promise not to forget," he smiled.

"How could I forget?" she murmured and felt Jack press her arm warmingly.

"Good girl," he said as they finally made their way to the bar. "The one thing an up-and-coming actress mustn't do is rebuff the attentions of her most influential angel."

"I'll clip his wings if he makes a pass at me!" she warned.

"You look far too angelic to harbor such thoughts." Jack signaled for drinks and, when the inevitable champagne was served, toasted her with his glass. "To the most exquisite girl in the room."

Alex raised her glass, and, at that moment, two women in front of her moved away and disclosed a group of people around a tall, wide-shouldered man.

Nicolas.

Nicolas, with his skin bronze against the whiteness of his shirt, with his hair black and shiny as a raven's wing. Alex's hand froze in midair, and she remained still as a statue. Nicolas was laughing at something, his head thrown back to disclose the thick column of his throat. Then he straightened, and, in doing so, his eyes stared directly into hers.

Taken by surprise, he had no chance to control his expression, and she saw his features stiffen into incredulity. Then his control took command, and his face became impassive. Casually, he turned his back on her, and Alex lowered her eyes and stared at the glass she was holding, marveling that her hand could be so steady when her entire body was trembling.

"Let's grab a table where we can eat," Jack said. "I don't know about you, but I'm starving."

The thought of food nauseated her, but she followed him to a table and made a pretence of choosing between fresh salmon and lobster, knowing that whatever she ate would taste like nothing to her.

"You never told me you knew Leon Panos," Jack said suddenly.

"It was a long time ago."

"He greeted you like a long-lost friend."

"We met when I was in France." She knew she had to say something more to appease Jack's curiosity. "I lost touch with him when I came back to England."

"It s just as well. He's a playboy, and you were wise not to get involved with him."

"You're presupposing he wanted to get involved."

"I can't imagine any man who wouldn't—with you."

She focused her attention on her plate, glad when several people whom Jack knew came over to join them. Out of the corner of her eye, she saw that Nicolas had moved away, and though some of her tension ebbed, her body was still tingling from the shock of seeing him. How soon could she induce Jack to leave? Not for another hour at least. The noise and the heat were becoming intolerable, and there was a throbbing in her temples that would become a first class headache if she did not take something to prevent it.

Murmuring that she was going in search of an aspirin, she wended her way through the tables towards the cloakroom. Admiring glances watched her progress, but her training as an actress stood her in good stead, and she was unembarrassed by them, though she breathed a sigh of relief when she reached the comparative calm of the hall.

There was a cool breeze here, and she stood for a moment enjoying it, her tiered skirt fluttering slightly. What a relief to be alone at last. Gathering up her skirts in one hand, she moved to the stairs, freezing into immobility as a man emerged from a room on her left.

"Hello, Alex," Nicolas said quietly.

She gave him a cool nod and went to glide past, but he stepped in front of her.

"Don't go. I want to talk to you."

"We've nothing to talk about."

"Maybe not," he said jerkily, "but I . . . . Don't go, Alex."

Short of pushing past him, she had no option but to stay where she was. His eyes moved slowly over her, from her softly flushed face to the quick rise and fall of her breasts, their movement causing a faint flutter of the frilly lace that half covered them. His eyes darkened, and his lower lip moved in a jerky, uncontrolled way.

"You are more beautiful than ever,' he said huskily.

She acknowledged the comment with a slight tilt of her head, and his own bent towards her. "You've had a great success in your play."

"You should come and see it."

"I saw it last night. You are an excellent actress."

"It wasn't all acting," she said coolly.

"Your speech where you say you will never fall in love."

"How clever of you to guess. But then you *are* clever at knowing what people mean, aren't you?"

"I have thought about you a great deal," he said inconsequentially.

"I've thought about you too," she said, still cool. "But only with regret."

He reddened, quickly and surprisingly, and it made her realize that until he had done so, his skin had been greyish despite its tan. He looked older than she remembered, and there were a deep line across his forehead and myriad small ones fanning out from his eyes. What was it Leon had said about him earlier? That he was working and playing like a demon? Her anger rose. There would never be a shortage of girls for Nicolas to love.

Her breathing quickened, and she caught at her skirts again. "Do you think you could let me pass?" she said. "I want to go upstairs."

For an instant, she had the impression he was going to refuse, then he stepped back and allowed her to move. Her foot was on the first step when she saw Elena coming down towards her. The last time they had met had been when the Greek-American had visited Nicolas for a brief while at the Clinic.

"Hello, Alex." Elena's greeting was warm. "I always say, if you go to enough of Dick's parties, you'll meet everyone you know!"

Alex managed to smile but for the life of her could not make any response. Luckily Elena did not seem to expect one, for she came down to the last step and slipped her hand through Nicolas's arm.

"Sorry to have kept you waiting, Nico, but I got waylaid by Tina."

"You know you love gossiping." There was tender amusement in his voice and, not waiting to hear more, Alex blindly hurried up the stairs.

Somehow or other, she managed to get through the rest of the evening, saying and doing the right things so that Jack did not notice anything amiss. It was dawn when he finally left her at her flat and suggested they meet for drinks later that day.

"Do you mind if I don't see you?" she replied. "I want to take it easy."

"I'm very easy!"

"Then prove it by giving in." She kissed him lightly on the cheek. "Good night, Jack. See you on Monday."

The door closed behind him, and she went listlessly into her bedroom, glad that Sherry was away for the weekend and there was no need for her to pretend any longer. She unhooked her dress and dropped it on to a chair. It lay there lifeless, as lifeless as she had been since she had seen Nicolas tonight.

Would he marry Elena? Remembering the affectionate way they had spoken to one another, it was logical to assume they might. Nicolas could well settle for such a marriage, for it would leave him free to pursue other *amours* when the mood took him. But she herself would never be one of those *amours*. She was part of a past he had sworn to forget. As she must forget.

She lay down and closed her eyes. "Dear God," she prayed. "Help me to stop thinking about him. Help me."

The persistent ringing of the doorbell awoke her from a heavy sleep, and wondering if it was Sherry returning unexpectedly, she stumbled out of bed to answer it. With the chain on, she peered through the door and saw Leon. He was ashen-faced, and his eyes were black pools of anxiety.

"Christ!" he gasped. "I thought you weren't in. I've been ringing for five minutes."

"I was asleep." She fumbled at the chain and opened the door wider. Only then did she take in his disheveled appearance and see he was still in evening clothes with a sweater carelessly covering his shirt.

"Why are you here?" she demanded.

"I've come to take you to Nico. He's had an accident."

She clutched at the back of a chair. "Is he badly hurt?"

"Yes. Hurry and get dressed. He's calling for you, Alex. I've promised to bring you."

Chapter
Fourteen

Like an automaton, Alex dressed, choosing the first thing that came to hand: sweater and skirt, the gossamer stockings she had worn last night, and black shoes that didn't match her brown bag. But what did her appearance matter when Nicolas was calling for her? When he might be dying?

"How did the accident happen?" she asked as she and Leon drove through the quiet London streets towards the Panos house in Kensington.

"He was injured in a mugging."

"A *what*"

"He saw somebody being mugged in a mews at the back of the house and went to help them. It must have been the first time in his life he ever went to get his own car from the garage, and *this* happened!"

"Was he on his own?"

"Yes. We'd got back from the party an hour earlier and had gone to bed. Heaven knows why Nico needed a car again—I never thought to find out. It was a miracle he managed to stagger back to the house after the fight. As it was, he passed out on the steps after ringing the bell. If his valet wasn't a light sleeper, he'd have been lying there till morning."

Leon swung the car into a private road dominated by foreign embassies and stopped outside one of the largest houses. Alex followed him up a flight of steps and into a huge hexagonal hall where Christoff Panos was waiting to greet them.

"Alex!" he said gruffly and held out his arms.

She ran into them, unaware of doing so until it was too late to draw back. His strong arms clasped her tightly, and a lined cheek was pressed against her own smooth one.

"Nico hasn't stopped calling for you. I will take you up at once."

"Is he badly hurt?" she asked as they mounted the stairs.

"He could have been killed. You know what these thugs are like. The man they attacked had to be taken to hospital, so at least Nico can count himself lucky."

Alex stopped walking. "It wasn't your idea to get me here, was it? If you're hoping for a reconciliation—"

"I never interfere in my son's private life," Christoff Panos interrupted. "I would like to, you understand, but Nico would never forgive me if I did."

"But if he isn't in hospital, he can't be so ill."

"He is ill enough to need you." Large hands shot out and pulled her none too gently down a corridor to a room at the end. He turned the handle and pushed her over the threshold. "Go in," he said and closed the door behind her.

Alex remained where she was, waiting for her heart to stop its erratic beating. The room was enormous and dominated by a king-size bed. In the midst of a sea of blue satin sheets, Nicolas lay motionless, his face pale as milk, his thick black hair partially covered by a bandage. The sight of him told her he had been severely mauled, and with a little cry she moved towards him.

Hearing the sound, he opened his eyes and saw her. "You came," he whispered. "I wasn't sure you would."

"Leon said—" Her mouth was so dry she had to moisten her lips before she could continue. "He said you were calling for me."

"Yes." He held out his hand. "Come closer. I can't see you properly."

She moved a step nearer and paused at the foot of his bed.

"Can't you bear to come closer than that?" he asked weakly. "Not that I blame you. When I remember the things I said to you . . . the way I behaved . . . . "

She shivered and resisted the urge to run away. "I hope you didn't bring me here to talk about the past."

"What else?" He struggled to sit up, and the effort brought beads of sweat to his forehead. "I've got to talk to you."

"Can't it wait? You're in pain, Nicolas; you should be resting."

"I cant rest until I've talked to you!" He sat up straighter, his face as white as his bandage. "You've got to forgive me, Alex. I'd give ten years of my life if I could wipe out that afternoon at the villa . . . the things I said to you. Say you forgive me!"

"Forgive you?" she echoed uncertainly.

"For doubting you! I've got my memory back, Alex. That blow on my head did it. I remember what happened at the cottage. Don't you understand what I'm trying to say?" He held out his hands. "Come close to me, darling. Let me hear you say you forgive me."

Shock rooted her to the spot. But even if her legs had obeyed her, they would have taken her as far away from Nicolas as possible.

"Darling," he whispered. "Come here."

"No! Never!"

The light drained from his eyes, turning them to dull black pebbles.

"So you still hate me. I'm not surprised. When I think of what I said to you! My only excuse is that I loved you so much, I went insane with jealousy. If I hadn't, I'd never have believed you capable of such behavior."

He pushed aside the bedclothes and tried to swing his feet to the ground. The exertion was too much for him, and he swayed and fell back against the pillows.

"Alex," he groaned. "I've never begged for anything in my life, but I'm begging you now. Say you forgive me."

"You've no need to beg."

Her voice was a thread of sound, and she could not go on. Many times in her dreams she had imagined Nicolas pleading with her like this. But in her dreams, she had flung his words at him. Yet now she could do so in reality, pity would not let her.

"Is it so hard for you to forgive?" he whispered.

"That's the easy part," she admitted shakily. "It's the forgetting that's impossible."

"I'll make you forget." His hands stretched toward her, but she recoiled from them.

"No, Nicolas. It won't work. I'll never be able to forget you didn't trust me. I'll always be afraid of doing or saying something that will make you doubt me again."

"I'll never doubt you."

"Not now, perhaps." She turned away. "But you will. It's no use, Nicolas. We can't go on where we left off."

"We can. We must!" His voice was slurred. "I love you. I want to marry you."

"No," she repeated firmly. "I'd never have any peace with you."

"You're not being logical." He pushed himself away from the pillows. "I love you, Alex. Don't you believe that?"

"You loved me before, but you doubted me. I begged you to have faith in me, but you refused to listen."

"Must I pay for that for the rest of my life?" he demanded.

"I'll have to pay, too."

"Neither of us need pay!" He caught at the bedside table to lever himself into a sitting position. "You can't walk out on me."

"Why not? We've both managed without each other

for months. I'm sure you'll soon fall in love with someone else."

"Have *you*?" His mouth twisted. "Is it your producer?"

"How quick you are to doubt me!" she cried. "You're doing exactly what I thought you would. You still don't trust me, and you never will!"

Not waiting to hear his answer, she ran from the room. She did not lessen her speed until she was half-way down the corridor, as though she were afraid Nicolas would suddenly find the strength to come after her. But it was illogical to be scared of a man who was too weak to get out of bed. The memory of his pale, bandaged face made her long to rush back and cradle him in her arms. Yet to do so would be a futile gesture that would lead to nothing except more heartbreak for them both. Blinking her eyes to clear them of tears, she went down to the hall.

"Miss Godfrey!" A sibilant voice called her name and Nicolas's valet came towards her with an envelope. "This is for you."

Puzzled, she took it and saw her name written in Nicolas's hand. "For me? But how——"

"Mr. Panos was holding it when I found him outside the house."

She frowned. "I don't understand."

"He was on his way to deliver it to you," the valet explained. "He came home from the party before everyone else and spent some time at his desk. I went in to see if he required anything, but he said he was going out to deliver a letter. I offered to take it, but he said he wished to go himself." The man hesitated. "He was on his way to the garage when he saw the other gentleman being attacked."

"When did you find him?" she asked jerkily.

"Half an hour later. He had collapsed on the steps by the back door. It's the one nearest to the mews. The letter was still in his hand."

Alex stared at the envelope and slowly tore it open. The valet moved away, and she took out a sheet of paper and began to read.

"When we parted in France," Nicolas began without any formality, "I went through all kinds of hell. I knew it wouldn't be easy to forget you, but I never realized I would miss you more and more each day.

"Seeing you tonight has confirmed what I've known for a long while—that I'll never stop loving you. If we hadn't met this evening, I would have come in search of you as soon as I had found the courage. Don't smile at my use of the word courage. For it would have taken a great deal of it to admit how badly I behaved to you. You aren't the type to give yourself lightly to a man, and you must have loved Leon very much. If you had told me the truth in the beginning, I would have brought him back from Greece and pushed him in front of the altar myself. But learning the truth the way I did made me so bitter that I lost my reason. What I'm trying to say is that if you had been honest with me when I first fell in love with you, I would either have made Leon marry you—if that were what you still wished—or have married you myself and taken care of the child.

"I wanted to tell you this at the party tonight, but I couldn't be clear-headed when I was near you. And

I've got to be clear-headed in order to make you understand how much I hate myself for what I did. Come back to me, Alex, and let's begin again. I'm bringing this letter to you myself, and I'll wait in the foyer while you read it. If you forgive me, press the elevator button. I will see it light up, and I will come to you."

His name was an indecipherable scrawl, as if he had reached the end of his control, as he undoubtedly must have done to have written such an impassioned plea.

The pages fluttered to the floor, and she picked them up and put them back into the envelope. Nicolas had written the letter before he had been attacked, *before his memory had returned.*

The implication of what this meant took a moment to sink in, but as it did, she began to tremble.

He had wanted her back when he had still believed it was Leon's child—and not his—that she had been carrying.

With a cry, she raced back up the stairs and down the corridor. At the bedroom door, she paused. Her fingers were so damp she could not turn the knob, and she rubbed them on her skirt and tried again. This time the door opened, and she stepped inside.

Nicolas was lying with his eyes closed. He had not heard her come in, and she tiptoed across to look at him. In repose, she saw how thin he was, and she noticed a sprinkle of grey in his hair that had not been there in the summer.

Gently, she reached out and touched his hand. Instantly his eyes opened. They were dark and clouded as though with pain, but as they saw her, they filled with light as if a lamp had been lit behind them.

"You came back," he said huskily.

"Yes."

With a murmur, she knelt by the bed and rested her head on his shoulder. Through the silk of his jacket she felt the pounding of his heart as, with a convulsive movement, he reached out and pulled her into his arms.

"Why did you come back, Alex?"

"Because of the letter. Your valet gave it to me. Why didn't you tell me you'd written it?"

"I don't know." He frowned. "It said nothing I didn't tell you a few moments ago."

"Of course it did! You wrote it before you got back your memory. You asked me to come back when you still thought Leon had been my lover."

Nicolas was silent as he slowly absorbed what she had said. "I should never have sent you away in the first place," he said thickly. "If I'd listened to my heart and not my head, I would have come after you the following day."

"You listened to your heart eventually," she whispered. "Your letter proved that."

"But only after I'd made both of us suffer for nothing. These past months have been a nightmare." His fingers wound themselves in the thick golden strands of her hair, and he pressed gentle kisses on her cheek and the side of her mouth. "I love you," he whispered. "I'll never let you go again."

Tenderly, she put her hand to his temple, careful

not to touch the bandage. "Don't talk any more, Nicolas, just hold me."

With a murmur that was almost a groan, he placed his mouth on hers. His lips were gentle and warm, growing less gentle as the feel of her mouth aroused him. Unwilling to excite him, she went to pull away, and he half smiled and tightened his hold.

"The only time I ever get you on my bed is when I have concussion!" he teased. "If I lose my memory this time, you must promise to tell me what I do."

"There'll be nothing to tell. I'm going to leave you in a moment. You must get some sleep."

"I've something else to say first." He pointed to the bureau by the far wall. "There's a special license in the top drawer. I've been carrying it round with me for days, summoning up the courage to come and see you. So all you have to do is set the day."

"The moment you're well enough." Tears shone in her eyes. "I want to be your wife so much that I'm—" She stopped, her elation ebbing as she remembered the play and her contract with Jack. Nicolas would never agree to share her with an audience each evening, and she was not sure she could manage more than a week's absence from the theater for a honeymoon.

"What's wrong?" he asked sharply.

"I'm not free. I've a run-of-the-play contract."

"So what?"

"So I'll have to be at the theater each night." She watched him carefully. "Won't you mind?"

"Not if it's what you want to do. You're a talented actress, darling, and if you want to continue your career, we'll arrange our lives accordingly."

"You'd hate sharing me with an audience," she said soberly. "Besides, you travel a lot, and I don't want to be parted from you."

He pulled farther away from her, the better to study her face. "What are you trying to tell me, my love?"

"That my marriage to you—the family we'll have— are more important to me than a career as an actress."

"Then I'll talk to Dick Liandris. He's the chief backer of your play, and if he tells your producer to release you, there'll be no problem."

She gave a wry smile. "The power of money."

"Does it worry you?"

"Not in this particular instance!" She hugged him. "We'll get married the minute you're well enough."

"When I hold you close, I'm already well."

The powerful surge that rushed through his body proved the truth of what he said, and she stood up quickly, coloring as she saw his teasing glance.

"This time next week you won't be able to escape me!" he said.

"I won't want to."

"Come close and repeat that."

"No." She backed to the door. "Go to sleep, darling. I'll be up to see you later."

With a sigh, he accepted defeat. "You won't disappear, will you? I'd hate to wake up and find it was all a dream."

"It's very real." She smiled and, giving way to temptation, moved back to the bed and kissed him again. "I love you, Nicolas. Keep remembering that, and you'll know it's no dream."

"I'll only know that for sure when you're my wife."

"Then hurry up and get well."

"I will," he promised. "You're the best incentive a man could have!"

Victoria Holt

*Here are the stories you love best. Tales about love,
intrigue, wealth, power and of course romance. Books
that will keep you turning the pages deep into the night*